Edge of Oblivion

Abiegail Rose

Staten House

Edge of Oblivion

In a world spiraling toward its final collapse, two people are forced to confront the ultimate decision as the apocalypse unfolds around them. Caleb, a man who has always trusted in logic and his own strength, watches helplessly as everything he once relied on crumbles into chaos. Rachel, driven by an unshakable hope, fights to endure, believing there's more at stake than survival alone.

As the world teeters on the edge of oblivion, every choice matters. One path leads to a chance at redemption, while the other spirals into ruin. In the midst of destruction, the future of humanity hangs in the balance, and the time for hesitation is over.

Edge of Oblivion is a gripping end-of-the-world saga, where fate, survival, and the power of choice determines who will endure—and who will fall.

The Revelation of Jesus Christ, which God gave unto him, to shew unto his servants things which must shortly come to pass; and he sent and signified *it* by his angel unto his servant John: [2] who bare record of the word of God, and of the testimony of Jesus Christ, and of all things that he saw. [3] *Blessed is he that readeth, and they that hear the words of this prophecy, and keep those things which are written therein: for the time is at hand.*

Revelation 1: 1-3

Defining Edge of Oblivion

Edge

edge *(noun)* · **edges** *(plural noun)*
- the outside limit of an object, area, or surface; a place or part farthest away from the center of something

- an area next to a steep drop

- *(the edge)* the point immediately before something unpleasant or momentous occurs or someone loses control

edge *(verb)*
- provide with a border or edge

- move gradually, carefully, or furtively in a particular direction

Oblivion

oblivion *(noun)*

- the state of being unaware or unconscious of what is happening

- the state of being forgotten, especially by the public

- extinction

law historical

- amnesty or pardon

Origin

- late Middle English: via Old French from Latin oblivio(n-), from oblivisci '**forget**'.

Edge of Oblivion Meaning

The phrase "edge of oblivion" can have two meanings:

1. To be on the knife-edge of being disregarded or forgotten

2. The point immediately before being granted amnesty or pardon

Dear Reader,

This is not just another story. *Edge of Oblivion* is a warning—a moment of reckoning at the very boundary between survival and extinction, where every decision takes you closer to the edge. As the world spirals toward its collapse, we stand at the outermost limits of what we once knew, staring into an uncertain future.

Edge of Oblivion speaks to the point where humanity teeters on the brink of oblivion—where one step further could mean being forgotten or lost forever, and another might offer the last chance for redemption. The time for indecision has passed. There is no longer space to stand between two choices, no fence to straddle. We are all moving, intentionally or not, toward a moment of irreversible consequence.

This story explores that exact moment, that fragile space between hope and destruction, where survival isn't just about making it through the end of the world but about the decisions that will determine who is remembered and who fades into oblivion. It is a reminder that waiting, ignoring the urgency of the choice before us, is the greatest danger of all.

I urge you to read *Edge of Oblivion* with a heart open to the weight of each decision. This story isn't just about a world ending; it's about the people within it, people like you and me, standing on the edge and deciding which way to turn—before the final step into oblivion is taken.

Sincerely,

Abiegail Rose
Author of *Edge of Oblivion*

1

The First Signs

Revelation 6: 1-2

The sky, once a dome of tranquil blue, was now streaked with red, as though a thousand unseen hands had smeared blood across the heavens. The air, heavy and thick with a strange tension, clung to the skin like damp cloth. Even the birds, whose songs usually filled the morning air, seemed to have grown silent, their absence as deafening as any scream.

In the distance, the rumbling of thunder echoed, though no storm approached. It was as if the earth itself shuddered, knowing what was to come, feeling the weight of something ancient stirring beneath its surface.

High above, a scroll prepared to be unsealed, invisible to the eyes of those on earth but seen clearly by the One who sat upon the throne. Seven seals bound it, each more significant than the last. It was no ordinary document. It held the fate of humanity—the culmination of all that had been foretold by the prophets, of things whispered in shadows and preached with trembling lips.

The time had come.

The first seal snapped open, the sound echoing through the chambers of heaven, a sound that resonated with power and finality. The figure who had broken it did so with authority, for only He was worthy to open the seals and read what was written. His face, obscured by light too bright for mortal eyes, radiated the strength of a lion and the gentleness of a lamb. The four living creatures, each with their own form and might, circled His throne, their voices raised in reverence as they cried out, "Come and see."

And behold, a rider emerged.

From the depths of heaven, he came, mounted on a white horse, gleaming and untarnished. The rider's presence was commanding, crowned with a victor's wreath. In his hand, he held a bow, though no arrows could be seen. He was not a mere soldier; he was a conqueror. His charge was not to wage war with bloodshed—not yet—but to subdue, to claim dominion over nations. And as he rode forward, the world would bow, some willingly, others in silent protest.

The rider galloped through the unseen veil between the heavens and the earth, his presence felt but not seen by those below. His conquest was subtle at first—a whisper among kings and rulers, a stirring among the people. One nation would rise in power, not through brute force but through cunning diplomacy and subtle manipulation. Leaders, once thought strong, would falter, their kingdoms crumbling without a single shot fired.

And still, the people below went about their days, unaware of the changes unraveling beneath their feet. They did not see the rider in white, nor did they hear the sound of the first seal breaking. But the earth knew. Creation itself trembled, knowing that the time of reckoning had begun. The heavens mourned, but the scroll would not be closed.

One by one, the seals would open. Each one would bring its own tribulation, its own horror, and its own test of faith. Those who had ears to hear and eyes to see would know. They would feel it deep in their souls, a gnawing sense of dread mingled with a flicker of hope. For to the faithful, these were not merely the signs of destruction, but the herald of a new beginning.

But for the others, the seals would be nothing more than a prelude to fear.

2

Rising Tensions

Caleb stared at the flickering screen of his TV, his thumb absentmindedly tapping the remote in his other hand. The news anchor's voice droned on, too calm for the panic that seemed to bubble beneath the surface of her words. Another protest in the streets, another election scandal overseas, another nation claiming sovereignty where it had none.

It was all just noise. The kind of chaos that had been creeping in for years, the kind that was easy to ignore if you didn't care enough to look too closely. Caleb had long ago stopped caring. Politics, wars, power grabs—it was all the same to him. He leaned back against the worn cushions of his couch, eyes half-closed as the newscaster rattled off numbers about inflation rates that seemed to climb by the hour.

> "Authorities in Europe report that leaders of six nations have resigned within the last month amid growing unrest. Economists warn that global markets may—"

Caleb snorted and muted the TV. It was always the same. The world felt like it was teetering on the edge, but it had felt that way for as long as he could remember. Every day, some new headline about the next big disaster or financial collapse, yet the sky didn't fall, and life went on. He'd heard people whispering about the "end times" since he was a kid, and none of it had ever amounted to anything more than conspiracy theories and fear-mongering.

The world was messed up, sure, but it wasn't ending. Not yet.

His phone buzzed on the coffee table, the screen lighting up with a text from his mom. She was a worrier, always checking in to make sure he wasn't caught up in whatever new disaster the news was hyping up. He picked it up, swiping to unlock.

Mom: *Saw the news about the protests. You staying safe?*

Caleb rolled his eyes but smiled despite himself. She lived three states away, but still acted like he was down the street and she could swoop in to protect him from whatever crisis loomed.

Caleb: *I'm fine, Mom. It's just more people freaking out about stuff that doesn't matter.*

He stared at the screen, waiting for her inevitable barrage of follow-up questions. But as the minutes passed in silence, Caleb found himself flipping through his own thoughts.

The protests were getting closer. The videos online showed more than just a handful of people holding signs. The streets were packed—crowds angry, shouting, pushing back against lines of police in riot gear. Something in those videos felt different. There was a hunger in the faces of those people, an intensity that hadn't been there in years past. It was as if everyone was on edge, waiting for something to give, for something to finally break.

He rubbed the back of his neck, a slow tension creeping into his muscles. The neighborhood had been quiet for now, just the usual city noise of traffic, dogs barking, kids playing. But even that seemed muted these days. The hum of life that used to fill the air had dimmed. Caleb wasn't sure when it started. He just knew that things felt...off.

He got up from the couch, pacing toward the window of his cramped apartment. Pulling the curtain aside, he peered down at the street below. A few cars rolled by, headlights cutting through the fading evening light. The corner market was still open, a handful of people moving in and out like it was any other night. Normal. Completely normal.

And yet, it didn't feel normal.

A strange stillness hung in the air, like the world was holding its breath. The hairs on the back of Caleb's neck stood up, prickling with unease. He clenched his fists at his sides, pushing the feeling down. It was ridiculous to think anything was different. The world had always been a mess, always on the verge of collapse, but it never actually collapsed.

He let the curtain fall back into place and turned away from the window, forcing a breath from his lungs. There was no reason to let it get to him. He grabbed his keys from the coffee table and shoved them into his pocket. He needed air, a distraction—anything to shake this weird feeling.

As he headed for the door, his phone buzzed again. Another message.

Mom: *Just be careful, okay? There's a lot going on. People are saying these are signs... You know, like what the Bible says about the end.*

Caleb scoffed, shaking his head as he locked his apartment door behind him. His mom had always been religious, the kind of person who saw God's hand in every little thing. He couldn't count how many times she'd told him about the Book of Revelation, about wars and rumors of wars, about the seals and the horsemen. It was all just old stories, fairy tales meant to keep people in line.

Caleb: *Mom, I'm not worried about some Bible prophecy. The world's just being the world. It's a mess, but it's not the end.*

He hit send and slipped the phone into his pocket, heading down the stairs and out onto the street. The air was cooler than it had been all day, but even the breeze didn't seem to shake the feeling that something was just...wrong. His steps echoed a little too loudly as he walked, the normal sounds of the city somehow quieter, more distant.

Maybe it was just him. Maybe he'd been watching too much news, letting all the doomsday talk seep into his head. People were always looking for something to be afraid of.

Still, as he walked past the closed-up shops and the flickering streetlights, that unsettling feeling lingered.

3

Signs of the Times

Rachel sat in the back pew of Everbrook Church, her Bible open on her lap, though her eyes weren't on the pages. The words of Pastor James echoed softly through the sanctuary, but her mind was elsewhere, caught in the threads of unease that had been weaving themselves into her thoughts for weeks now.

She shifted in her seat, her fingers tracing over the familiar worn edges of her Bible. The world outside the church felt like it was tilting, like the foundations were cracking, but in here, there was stillness. A calm before the storm. The soft glow of the stained glass windows cast colored patterns across the floor, painting everything in muted reds and blues as the sun began to set outside.

"Now, I know many of you have been watching the news," Pastor James said, his voice steady but urgent. "It seems like everywhere we turn, there's chaos. Nations are rising against each other, disasters we can't explain, economies faltering. But we, as believers, know this is not unexpected. The Bible warned us these days would come."

Rachel glanced around the sanctuary. Most of the seats were filled, more than usual for a midweek service. People seemed to be drawn in by something, even if they couldn't fully articulate what it was. She saw it in their faces—the quiet anxiety, the nervous fidgeting of hands, the looks exchanged between friends and family. They felt it too, the tension in the air, the creeping sensation that the world was changing in ways that no one could quite understand.

She knew what it was. She had known for a long time.

Her fingers stopped tracing the pages, resting on a passage she had marked months ago.

> **Matthew 24:7**: *"For nation shall rise against nation, and kingdom against kingdom: and there shall be famines, and pestilences, and earthquakes, in divers places."*

The words, once abstract in their prophecy, had started to feel very real.

Pastor James continued, his voice growing more impassioned. "We are living in the last days, brothers and sisters. The signs are all around us, and as the people of God, we must be prepared. We must keep our eyes open, our hearts ready, because His return could come at any moment."

Rachel felt a shiver run down her spine, though it wasn't fear that gripped her. It was something deeper—an anticipation that had been building within her, growing stronger with each passing day. The world was unraveling, yes, but this was what had to happen. It was all part of the plan, the grand design laid out in the scriptures. The seals were breaking, one by one, and each fracture brought them closer to the end.

She looked over at her friend Sarah, sitting next to her, flipping anxiously through her own Bible. Rachel could see the fear in her eyes, the uncertainty. Sarah hadn't grown up in the church the way Rachel had; her faith was still new, fragile, like a young tree trying to take root in rocky soil. She was scared, and Rachel couldn't blame her. The things happening in the world weren't easy to understand, even for someone who had been studying the Bible her whole life.

Rachel leaned over, touching Sarah's arm gently. "It's going to be okay," she whispered. "We knew this was coming."

Sarah nodded, but her eyes betrayed her. "It just feels so...real now. Like it's not just something we talk about in Bible study anymore."

"I know," Rachel said softly. "But that's why we need to stay strong. This is what we've been preparing for. God's in control."

Sarah nodded again, but the tension in her shoulders didn't ease. Rachel felt a pang of empathy. It was one thing to know the prophecies, to believe them in theory. It was another thing entirely to watch them unfold in real time.

Pastor James paused for a moment, letting the weight of his words settle over the congregation. The church was silent, save for the occasional shuffle of feet or a soft cough. Outside, the wind picked up, rattling the old windows slightly, as if the earth itself was listening.

"We don't know the exact day or hour," Pastor James continued, his voice softer now, more solemn, "but we are commanded to be watchful. The signs are there for us to see, and we must not be caught unprepared. The world is going to look for answers in all the wrong places. They'll look to politicians, to wealth, to science, but none of that can save them from what's coming."

Rachel's chest tightened. She thought of Caleb, her old friend from high school. They hadn't spoken much since they'd gone their separate ways after graduation, but they still ran into each other from time to time. He was a good person—smart, thoughtful in his own way—but he'd never believed in the things she did. Whenever the topic of faith came up, he'd brush it off with a joke or a shrug, like it was some distant thing that didn't concern him.

She had tried to talk to him about what was happening, about the signs, but he wouldn't hear it. He laughed it off, called it paranoia. But Rachel could see it in his eyes—the doubt, the fear he tried to mask with sarcasm. She prayed for him, every night. She prayed that his heart would soften, that he'd see the truth before it was too late. Because she knew, deep down, that the time was running out.

Pastor James's voice broke through her thoughts again. "We are not called to fear, but to faith. We are not called to confusion, but to trust. God has not abandoned us, and He will not. But we must hold fast, no matter what comes next."

The service ended quietly, people gathering their belongings in a kind of hushed reverence, as though they had been let in on a secret too heavy to speak aloud. Rachel stood, closing her Bible gently and slipping it into her bag. She turned to Sarah and smiled, trying to project a calm she didn't fully feel.

"Do you want to grab coffee later this week?" Rachel asked, hoping a little normalcy might help settle Sarah's nerves.

Sarah smiled weakly. "Yeah, I'd like that."

They walked out of the church together, the cool evening air biting at their skin. The streets were quiet, the sun dipping below the horizon, casting long shadows across the town. Rachel pulled her coat tighter around her shoulders as they parted ways, her thoughts drifting back to Caleb. She would reach out to him again tomorrow, try once more to get him to listen.

As she walked home, the unease she had felt earlier returned, settling in the pit of her stomach. But it wasn't fear—it was more like a weight, a sense of gravity pulling her toward something inevitable. The world was shifting, the seals breaking, and there was no turning back.

She looked up at the darkening sky, the first few stars beginning to pierce through the fading light. Somewhere, out there, things were happening—things that had been written long before she was born. And she knew, with a certainty that ran deeper than the unease, that they were living through the beginning of the end.

4

The Next Seals

Revelation 6:3-6

The earth quivered in silence, a foreboding pause that seemed to stretch over the heavens. Far beyond the reach of mortal eyes, the second seal was broken. It wasn't a sound that could be heard, but it echoed through the universe, stirring something ancient and powerful. The moment the seal snapped, a second rider appeared, called forth by the same living creature who had witnessed the first.

"Come and see."

And behold, a horse, its color the deep, violent red of spilled blood, surged forward from the heavens. The rider was armed with a great sword, his eyes burning with the fury of nations. Unlike the first, this rider's mission was not subtle or concealed. His charge was clear: to take peace from the earth, to fan the flames of war until they consumed everything in their path.

The sword gleamed in his hand, shimmering with an ominous light as he descended toward the earth. Below, onlookers went about their daily lives, unaware of the storm gathering above them. But the earth knew. The earth had always known. It trembled beneath the rider's hooves as he crossed the unseen boundary between the heavenly and the earthly realms.

Nations, already teetering on the brink, now felt the full force of the rider's influence. In capitals and parliaments, tempers flared, alliances shattered, and leaders, gripped by unseen hands, made decisions they would soon regret. The sound of marching feet echoed through streets once filled with laughter, the rumble of tanks and the clatter of weapons drowned out the cries for peace.

Across the globe, conflict erupted. Not the quiet, simmering kind that had lingered for years, but open, violent war that tore apart families, cities, and countries. There was no safe place, no corner of the earth untouched by the rider's fury. Blood soaked the ground, and the people, who had once believed they were above such madness, now found themselves swept up in its destructive tide.

In the skies above, the rider in red pressed onward, relentless in his task. Peace had been removed, and what followed was the darkest side of humanity, laid bare for all to see.

As the rider's influence spread, the earth itself seemed to groan under the weight of his passing. The world knew—creation itself knew—that this was only the beginning. There were more seals to be broken, more riders yet to come.

But for now, the second horseman rode on, leaving a trail of devastation in his wake.

And still, the heavens were not silent.

5

The World Falls Apart

Caleb paced back and forth in his apartment, his phone in his hand, refreshing the news feed over and over again. It didn't make sense. None of it made sense. Every headline that flashed across the screen was worse than the last—violence erupting in cities across Europe, governments falling, wars breaking out over borders that had stood unchallenged for decades.

He stopped in front of the window, pressing his palm against the glass, his breath fogging the cool surface. Outside, his usually quiet street was unusually busy. Neighbors were gathered in tight clusters, talking in hushed tones, their faces tight with worry. The grocery store down the block had a line stretching around the corner, people with carts full of water, canned goods, and everything they could grab. The sense of panic had spread like a virus.

He turned away from the window, unable to stand the sight of it all. What was happening? How had things fallen apart so fast? It felt like the world had been fine just days ago. There were always problems—he knew that—but nothing like this. The headlines swirled in his mind, each one more absurd than the next.

> *Civil unrest sweeps across Europe.*

> *Border disputes turn deadly in the Middle East.*

> *Government officials resign en masse as nations brace for war.*

Caleb tossed his phone onto the couch, running both hands through his hair, the tension in his body building with every passing second. His mind raced, searching for some rational explanation, but it kept coming up short. There was no logic to it. Sure, the world had its fair share of issues, but global collapse? He couldn't wrap his head around it.

The news anchors didn't have any answers either. They were just as lost as everyone else, scrambling to make sense of the chaos, trying to spin the facts into something that felt manageable, something that people could process. But Caleb didn't buy it. There was no managing this. It was too big, too sudden.

His stomach growled, reminding him that he hadn't eaten since breakfast. With a sigh, he wandered into the kitchen, but the sight of the half-empty fridge did little to ease the pit in his gut. The shelves were sparse, and he knew going to the store now would be a nightmare. He'd seen the lines. It looked like people were preparing for the apocalypse, and maybe they were.

He grabbed a can of soup from the cupboard, popped it open, and stood there in the kitchen, eating it cold, straight from the can. He barely tasted it, his mind too preoccupied with everything unraveling outside his door.

A soft vibration caught his attention—his phone buzzing again. Caleb wiped his hand on his jeans and grabbed it from the couch.

Mom: *Caleb, are you okay? I've been watching the news. It's so scary out there. I'm praying for you.*

He stared at the screen, his jaw tightening. His mom. Always with the prayers. Always with the faith. She couldn't just call him like a normal person, couldn't just ask him how he was and leave it at that. No, she had to turn it into something religious, something spiritual.

Caleb typed a quick response:

I'm fine, Mom. Just busy. Don't worry.

He hesitated, hovering over the send button, but the words felt hollow even to him. He wasn't fine, and she had every right to be worried. But what was the point in telling her that? What could she do from hundreds of miles away? Pray more?

He sent the message, tossing the phone back onto the couch and slumping down beside it. The weight of everything pressing down on him felt suffocating. His mind wandered to Rachel again, her calm, almost unnerving certainty that all of this was just...expected. She had warned him. He couldn't forget that. He hadn't wanted to hear it at the time, had laughed it off when she started talking about the Bible and prophecies, but now...

Now, her words kept creeping into the corners of his mind, no matter how hard he tried to push them out.

He grabbed the remote, turning the TV back on, needing the distraction. The screen flickered to life, showing scenes from another protest—this time in the U.S. Crowds of people clashed with police in riot gear, tear gas hanging in the air like a ghostly cloud. The camera zoomed in on a man shouting into a mega-phone, his voice rising above the chaos.

> *"This is what happens when the government fails us!"* the man screamed, his voice hoarse. *"They've abandoned us! They've left us to fight for ourselves!"*

The crowd surged, fists in the air, and Caleb felt his heart begin to race. It was all spinning out of control. He switched the channel, but the next news station was no better. Images of sol-diers marching in the Middle East filled the screen, followed by a grim-faced reporter talking about escalating violence between rival factions.

He couldn't take it anymore. Caleb turned the TV off, sinking back into the couch, pressing the heels of his hands into his eyes. This wasn't how things were supposed to be. This wasn't how the world worked.

He thought of the empty shelves in the store, the people hoard-ing supplies, the lines stretching for blocks. It was like they all knew something he didn't, like they were preparing for the end of everything. But that wasn't possible. People didn't just wake up one day and start acting like it was the end of the world.

Or did they?

His mind raced back to Rachel again, to the warning she had tried to give him a few weeks ago. She had sounded so sure of herself, so convinced that all of this chaos was part of some bigger plan, that it had been foretold. He had laughed it off, brushed her aside with some sarcastic comment about conspiracy theories.

But now, sitting here, alone in his apartment while the world seemed to burn outside, Caleb wasn't so sure.

A knock on the door startled him. Caleb jerked upright, his heart pounding in his chest. Who would be here now? He wasn't expecting anyone. Slowly, he stood, crossing the room to the door. Peering through the peephole, he saw his neighbor, an older woman who lived two floors down.

He unlocked the door and opened it a crack.

"Hey," she said, her voice shaky. "Sorry to bother you, but...have you heard anything? The news is saying there might be more protests downtown, and...I don't know. I just don't feel safe right now. Do you?"

Caleb swallowed hard. He wanted to tell her everything would be fine, that things were going to calm down, but the words stuck in his throat. He didn't feel safe either, not anymore.

"I don't know," he said honestly. "I'm just trying to figure it out like everyone else."

She nodded, her lips pressed into a thin line. "Yeah. Me too."

They stood there in awkward silence for a moment before she gave him a tight smile and turned to leave.

As Caleb closed the door, he felt that familiar knot of anxiety tighten in his chest. The world was falling apart, and no one knew why. Everyone was scrambling, trying to make sense of the senseless.

He sat back down on the couch, his thoughts spinning. Maybe Mom and Rachel weren't so crazy after all.

6

HOLDING ON TO FAITH

Rachel sat at her kitchen table, her Bible spread open before her, the pages marked with notes scribbled in the margins. The late afternoon sunlight filtered in through the curtains, casting a warm glow across the room. But despite the warmth, Rachel could feel the chill creeping into her heart, the unease that seemed to hang in the air like a storm waiting to break.

She had always known these days would come. Ever since she was a little girl, sitting in Sunday school, she had heard the stories—prophecies about wars, earthquakes, famine, and pestilence. They had always seemed like distant, abstract things, events that might happen long after her lifetime. But now, as she flipped through the familiar pages of scripture, the words felt different. They felt like they were breathing, like they were alive, wrapping around her like the wind before a storm.

> *"For nation shall rise against nation, and kingdom against kingdom: and there shall be famines, and pestilences, and earthquakes, in divers places."*

The words of Matthew 24 were etched into her heart, but now they echoed with a clarity that made her skin prickle. The headlines on the news, the unrest spilling into the streets, the whispers in the church—they were all pointing to the same thing. The world was shifting, changing in ways that were hard to explain, but impossible to ignore.

She closed her Bible, resting her hands on the cover for a moment, letting out a slow breath. The unease that had settled in her chest wasn't fear—at least, not the kind of fear that left her paralyzed. It was more like...urgency. A sense of knowing that things were going to get worse before they got better, but that there was a purpose behind it all. God's hand was in this, even if it was hard to see right now.

Her phone buzzed on the table beside her Bible, and she glanced at the screen.

Text from Sarah:

Rach, have you seen the news today? It's getting worse. I don't know what to do. Call me when you can.

Rachel's heart sank a little as she read the message. Sarah had been struggling for weeks now, ever since the first wave of protests and unrest had hit the news. Her faith was still so new, still so fragile, and Rachel could see the cracks forming. She knew Sarah was scared, and Rachel had tried her best to be there, to remind her of the promises they held onto as believers. But the weight of the world's chaos was heavy, even for someone as strong in faith as Rachel.

She texted back quickly:

I'll call you in a bit. It's going to be okay. Hang in there.

Rachel set the phone aside and stood, moving to the window. The view from her small apartment wasn't much—a narrow street below, a few trees lining the sidewalk, the edges of downtown visible in the distance. But even from here, she could feel the tension in the city. There was a heaviness, an underlying current of fear that seemed to hum through the air. It was as if everyone was holding their breath, waiting for the next thing to go wrong.

The news had been relentless—stories of violence breaking out in the streets, governments collapsing, people fleeing their homes in fear. And it wasn't just happening far away anymore. It was here, in their own country, their own city. Every day, Rachel saw it—on the faces of people at the grocery store, in the worried glances exchanged at church. It was everywhere.

But even in the midst of the chaos, Rachel felt an undeniable sense of peace, a calm that anchored her to the truth she had known all her life. God had not abandoned them. He had not abandoned her.

She turned from the window and walked back to the kitchen, her fingers brushing over the edge of the Bible on the table. The words inside it had always been her guide, her compass, and now more than ever, they were her lifeline.

Her phone buzzed again, and this time, Rachel smiled softly when she saw the name on the screen.

Mom: *Praying for you today, sweetheart. Don't forget He's with us, no matter what. Isaiah 41:10.*

Her mom had always been her biggest spiritual influence, always reminding her to turn to scripture when the world felt overwhelming. Rachel didn't need to look up the verse—she knew it by heart.

> *"Fear thou not; for I am with thee: be not dismayed; for I am thy God: I will strengthen thee; yea, I will help thee; yea, I will uphold thee with the right hand of my righteousness."*

Rachel's smile grew as she texted back a quick thank you. It was a simple verse, one she had read a hundred times, but right now, it felt like a lifeline. The world was falling apart, but God's promises hadn't changed. They never would.

She needed to talk to Sarah, to reassure her that they were going to get through this. But first, she needed a moment to gather her thoughts, to pray. She could feel the weight of the day pressing down on her shoulders, and she knew she couldn't face it without turning to God first.

Rachel moved to the small corner of her living room where she had set up a quiet space for prayer. The old armchair by the window had become her sanctuary in recent months, a place where she could sit and be still, even when everything around her felt like it was spinning out of control.

She sank into the chair, folding her hands in her lap, and closed her eyes. The city hummed outside, the distant sounds of traffic and voices filtering through the window. But here, in this moment, it was quiet. Peaceful.

"Father," she whispered, her voice soft but steady, "I know You're in control. I know You've already seen the end of this story, and I trust You. But it's hard right now. It's hard to see the world breaking apart and not feel the weight of it. Help me to hold on to Your promises, and help me to be a light for those around me."

She paused, taking a deep breath, her hands tightening together.

"I pray for Sarah," she continued. "I know she's scared, and I know she's struggling. Give me the words to comfort her, to remind her that You haven't left us. Help her to feel Your presence, even in the chaos."

Another pause, another breath.

"And...I pray for Caleb."

The words were harder this time. Caleb had always been in her prayers, but lately, it felt more urgent. The last time she had seen him, he had been so dismissive, so sure that everything was just another cycle of bad news. He didn't see what she saw. He didn't understand the bigger picture. But Rachel couldn't shake the feeling that he was closer to seeing the truth than he realized.

"I know You love him," she whispered. "I know You're reaching out to him, even if he doesn't see it yet. Soften his heart. Open his eyes. And give me the courage to keep trying, to keep showing him the truth, even when he doesn't want to hear it."

Rachel sat in silence for a long moment, letting the quiet wash over her, letting the weight of her prayers settle. When she finally opened her eyes, the sun had dipped lower, casting longer shadows across the room. She felt a little lighter, a little more grounded.

There was so much she didn't understand, so much she couldn't control. But here, in this small space, with her Bible and her prayers, she knew one thing for sure: she wasn't alone.

God was with her.

And no matter what came next, that would be enough.

7

The Pale Horse

Revelation 6:7-8

The heavens stirred again, an invisible hand drawing open the third seal. Its opening was silent, but the world beneath felt its weight. The ground trembled with anticipation, a low murmur of unrest spreading across nations. And from the unseen realms, a third rider emerged.

"Come and see," the voice of the living creature thundered once more, the command echoing across the stars.

And behold, the Pale Horse appeared, its rider gaunt and hollow, his form shrouded in the sickly color of decay. His presence carried the stench of death, his skeletal fingers clutching a set of scales, their balance uneven. He rode forth not with the triumphant gait of a conqueror or the fierce speed of a warrior, but with a slow, deliberate pace, as if savoring the ruin he would soon bring.

Wherever he rode, the land beneath him withered. Crops shriveled in their fields, rivers turned to dust, and the beasts of the earth staggered under the weight of their hunger. Famine followed in his wake, spreading across cities and villages like a plague, sparing none who walked the earth.

The scales in his hands tipped, and a voice from the midst of the four living creatures called out, "A measure of wheat for a penny, and three measures of barley for a penny; and see thou hurt not the oil and the wine."

It was a proclamation of scarcity, a warning that the time of plenty had passed. The earth would no longer yield its abundance, and the people would toil for the barest of sustenance. The luxuries of oil and wine, reserved for the wealthy, would remain, but for the common man, survival itself would be an agonizing struggle.

The Pale Rider's horse stamped its hooves, the sound hollow and haunting, as it carried him forward. Below, unseen, the world bent beneath the weight of famine and death. Markets crumbled, and the clamor of merchants faded into quiet despair. The fields that once ripened with golden grain now lay barren, reduced to dust beneath the rider's steady march.

His mission was clear, his presence felt across every corner of the earth, and still, more destruction loomed in the distance.

The Pale Horse had come, and with it, hunger, loss, and despair.

8

Personal Loss

The air in Caleb's apartment was suffocating, thick with the stale scent of untouched food and the heavy silence that seemed to cling to everything. He sat at his kitchen table, the cold surface pressing into his arms as he stared at his phone, willing it to ring. His thoughts spun in circles, circling the same unanswered questions, the same creeping dread he had been trying to suppress for days.

He scrolled through the news feeds again, but the words blurred together, the headlines a jumbled mess of disaster after disaster. The constant stream of bad news had become almost unbearable—markets collapsing, riots spreading like wildfire, entire regions struggling with famine. What had once seemed like distant problems, things happening to other people, now felt closer than ever.

The world wasn't just in turmoil anymore—it was unraveling.

Caleb's fingers twitched, his thoughts drifting to the last conversation he'd had with his sister. He'd called her a few days ago, trying to check in after he saw the news about the food shortages in her area. She had brushed it off, trying to sound optimistic, but he had heard the strain in her voice. He'd told her to stock up, to be careful, to avoid the crowds that were growing more desperate by the day.

Now, he hadn't heard from her in over forty-eight hours.

The gnawing pit in his stomach deepened as he tried to call her again. The dial tone buzzed in his ear, and for a moment, he thought she might pick up, that her familiar voice would cut through the silence. But the line went dead—again. His heart sank, a tight knot of panic rising in his chest.

He slammed the phone down, the sharp sound breaking the stillness of the apartment. Leaning forward, he buried his face in his hands, trying to push back the panic that had been creeping closer with every passing hour. It wasn't like her to go quiet. Not like this. Not when things were getting so bad.

He forced himself to stand, pacing the length of the room, his footsteps echoing off the walls. The apartment felt too small, too stifling. Outside, the street was unusually quiet—no kids playing, no casual conversations drifting through the air. Even the traffic seemed muted, as if the city itself was holding its breath.

Caleb moved to the window and pulled the curtain aside, his eyes scanning the street below. The grocery store at the corner had its lights off, a hand-painted sign taped to the door that read *Closed Until Further Notice.* The small crowd that had been lining up outside days ago was gone, replaced by the eerie stillness of an abandoned storefront. He had been down there a few times himself, trying to pick up basic supplies, but the shelves were as empty as his own cabinets.

He hadn't realized how quickly things could fall apart. The hunger was starting to settle in now—not just his, but everywhere. He could see it on the faces of the few people who still wandered the streets. They moved slower, their eyes hollow, their bodies thin from days of stretching what little food they had left.

Caleb's mind raced, thinking back to the conversations he had dismissed, the warnings he had ignored. Rachel had been right there, in front of him, trying to tell him something that he hadn't wanted to hear. He remembered the quiet concern in her eyes, the way her voice had softened when she talked about the signs she saw. He had laughed it off, chalking it up to religious hysteria. But now, the world outside his window was starting to look like the very thing she had warned him about.

His phone buzzed on the table, pulling him from his thoughts. He snatched it up, his heart jumping into his throat when he saw his sister's name flash on the screen. For a brief second, relief surged through him. But when he answered, it wasn't her voice he heard.

"Caleb?" It was her husband, Derek, his voice strained and raw.

"Derek, what's going on? Is she okay?" Caleb's words tumbled out, his grip tightening on the phone.

There was a long pause on the other end, and in that silence, Caleb felt something heavy settle in his chest. He could hear the weight of Derek's breathing, the hesitation, and knew before he spoke what the answer would be.

"She's gone, Caleb." Derek's voice cracked. "The doctors...t hey couldn't do anything. The hospital's overwhelmed. There's not enough food, not enough medicine... She's gone."

Caleb staggered back, the words hitting him like a physical blow. His mind refused to process it, refused to make sense of what he was hearing. The room spun, and he sank into a chair, his legs giving out beneath him.

"No...no, that's... How?" His voice was barely more than a whisper.

"She was already weak... She hadn't been eating enough. They said...they said it was pneumonia, but the truth is, she just...she couldn't fight it anymore." Derek's voice cracked again, choking on the words. "We tried, Caleb. We really did."

Caleb's throat tightened, and he pressed a hand to his forehead, feeling the cold sweat that had started to form. The world outside felt distant, muted, as if it no longer existed. All that remained was the crushing weight of those two words.

She's gone.

The phone slipped from his hand, falling to the floor with a dull thud. His sister. His only sister. Gone. The world felt as though it was collapsing in on itself, every terrible thing that had seemed so far away now crashing down around him. The famine, the shortages, the wars—they weren't just things he watched on a screen anymore. They were real. They had taken something from him.

He hadn't even been there.

Caleb sat motionless, his mind spinning in circles, his heart pounding in his chest. His thoughts drifted again to Rachel, to her warnings about what was coming. For the first time, he let himself wonder if maybe, just maybe, she had been right. Maybe there was something more to all of this. Maybe the world wasn't just breaking apart—it was being judged.

But even as the thought crossed his mind, Caleb shoved it down, refusing to let it take hold. He couldn't believe that. He wouldn't. There had to be another explanation. This couldn't be part of some divine plan. It couldn't be.

Yet, as the silence stretched on, the empty space where his sister's voice should have been echoed louder than anything else.

Outside, the wind picked up, swirling dust through the empty streets, as if the world itself was mourning.

9

The Faithful Endure

Rachel knelt by the side of her bed, her Bible open in front of her, its pages rippling slightly in the breeze that slipped in through the cracked window. The apartment was quiet, almost too quiet, but the stillness felt like a balm to her soul. Outside, the world was falling apart, but here, in this small corner of her home, there was peace. She closed her eyes, hands resting on the worn edges of the Bible, and let the silence linger, focusing her heart on the prayer that had been rising in her mind all morning.

"Father, give us strength," she whispered, her voice steady, though her body trembled slightly. "I know You see everything. You see the hurt, the fear... You see what's happening in the streets. But I trust You, Lord. Even when it's hard. Even when the world feels like it's breaking... I trust You."

She paused, her breath catching as the weight of her words settled over her. Trusting wasn't the hard part. Trusting was what she had been doing her whole life. It was the waiting—the waiting for God's hand to move, for His promises to be fulfilled—that weighed heavy on her heart. But she held onto her faith like a lifeline, knowing that this storm, like all others, would pass in His time.

Her phone buzzed softly beside her, and Rachel opened her eyes, glancing at the screen. A text from her mother. She reached for it, her fingers brushing the edges of the Bible as she picked up the phone.

Mom: *Praying for you today, sweetie. Hold on to the promises. He's always faithful.*

Rachel smiled, the warmth of her mother's words sinking into her heart. Her mom had always known exactly what to say, always knew how to remind her of the truth she needed to hear. And right now, those words felt like they were the only thing keeping her tethered to hope.

She stood, tucking her Bible under her arm as she walked to the window. The sky outside was a dull gray, heavy clouds rolling across it in thick, slow-moving waves. The street below, usually alive with the chatter of neighbors and children playing, was quiet. The grocery store at the corner was still shuttered, its doors locked, the windows dark. A few people hurried past, their faces drawn and thin, moving with a kind of resigned determination that Rachel had seen too many times in recent weeks.

The famine had hit hard. Everywhere she looked, there were signs of it—the empty shelves, the rationing, the whispered conversations in church about families who couldn't make ends meet. Rachel had seen it in her own home too. Meals had grown smaller, and she found herself stretching what little food she had, rationing in ways she had never thought she'd need to. But even with the hunger, even with the fear that hovered over the city like a cloud, Rachel felt a strange calm.

She knew why.

Her faith had always been strong, but in these past few weeks, it had become unshakeable. She had seen the signs—the wars, the chaos, the famine—and she knew that these were not random events. These were the days the prophets had spoken of, the days that she had read about her entire life. And while the world around her seemed to be falling apart, Rachel saw something else. She saw a plan unfolding. A divine plan.

"Thank you, Lord," she whispered, her eyes still on the quiet street below. "Thank you for Your promises."

She could feel His presence with her, even now, as the world outside grew darker. And with that presence came a certainty that no matter how bad things got, no matter how much the earth shook or the skies darkened, God was still in control.

A knock at the door pulled her from her thoughts. Rachel turned, setting her Bible on the windowsill before crossing the small room to the door. When she opened it, she was greeted by the familiar face of Mrs. Henderson, one of the older women from her church. Her face was lined with worry, her gray hair pulled back into a loose bun, her hands wringing a fraying scarf between her fingers.

"Rachel, dear," Mrs. Henderson's voice trembled, "I—I didn't mean to disturb you, but..."

Rachel reached out, touching the woman's arm gently. "It's okay, Mrs. Henderson. Come in."

She stepped aside, and the older woman shuffled inside, her eyes darting around the room nervously. Rachel guided her to the kitchen table, pulling out a chair for her.

"Is everything alright?" Rachel asked softly as she sat down across from her, already knowing the answer.

Mrs. Henderson shook her head, her fingers tightening around the scarf. "I... I don't know what to do, Rachel. The food... the stores are empty. And my grandson... he's hungry. He hasn't eaten in two days. I... I don't know how much longer we can last."

Rachel's heart clenched at the woman's words, but she kept her face calm, steady. "We'll figure something out," she said, reaching for Mrs. Henderson's hands, holding them gently in her own. "You're not alone in this. We're going to get through it together."

Mrs. Henderson's eyes filled with tears, her voice cracking. "I've been praying, Rachel. I've been praying every night, but... it's so hard. It's hard to hold on when everything is falling apart."

Rachel squeezed her hands a little tighter. "I know it's hard. It feels like everything is shaking, like the world is breaking apart at the seams. But we have to remember that this isn't the end. It's just a chapter in the story. God hasn't left us. He's still with us, right here, in the middle of all this."

Mrs. Henderson nodded, her tears slipping down her cheeks, but Rachel could see the glimmer of hope returning to her eyes. She knew that feeling—the struggle to hold on, the fight to be-lieve when everything around you screamed that it was hopeless. But Rachel had learned long ago that faith wasn't about what she could see. It was about what she knew deep in her soul.

Rachel stood and moved to the small pantry in the corner of the kitchen. It wasn't much—just a few cans of soup, some rice, and a half-full jar of peanut butter—but she grabbed what she could.

She couldn't let Mrs. Henderson and her grandson go without. God would provide. He always had.

She placed the small offering of food into Mrs. Henderson's trembling hands. "Take this. It's not a lot, but it'll get you through a couple of days. We'll figure out the rest as we go."

Mrs. Henderson looked down at the food, her lips trembling with gratitude. "Oh, Rachel... thank you. You don't know what this means."

Rachel smiled gently, but inside, she felt a familiar warmth, a quiet assurance that they weren't alone in this. "God's going to take care of us," she said softly. "All of us."

After Mrs. Henderson left, Rachel closed the door and leaned back against it, letting out a slow breath. The weight of it all was heavy—heavier than she could carry on her own. But she wasn't carrying it alone. She had her faith, and that faith was her anchor, keeping her grounded even when the world threatened to pull her under.

She returned to the window, her eyes drifting back to the gray sky, the heavy clouds that lingered on the horizon. She didn't know what was coming next, but she knew one thing for sure.

The faithful would endure.

They had to.

10

The Fourth and Fifth Seals

Revelation 6:9-11

The heavens stirred once more, a ripple of divine power spreading through the realms as the Lamb broke the fourth seal. This time, the sound of its shattering seemed to shake the very foundation of the earth, though no human ear could hear it. But the world felt it—deep in the soil, in the air, in the hearts of those who wandered its surface. The final horseman had been summoned.

"Come and see," the voice of the living creature rang out again, a command as clear and unavoidable as the dawn.

And behold, a pale horse emerged from the unseen, its rider thin and skeletal, his form barely more than shadow and bone. Death clung to him like a shroud, and the name "Hades" followed in his wake, lingering in the air like a bitter chill. He held no weapon, for his mere presence was enough to bring destruction. The horse's hooves struck the ground, silent to the ears of man, but their impact was felt everywhere.

Where the other riders had left the world teetering on the edge of chaos, the pale rider pushed it over. As he galloped unseen across nations, the bodies of the fallen lined his path. Death was his calling card, and he brought it to the four corners of the earth—through famine, through plague, through war. The land gave no sustenance; what little remained was guarded fiercely, stolen or hoarded. The weak fell first, crumbling beneath the weight of hunger, disease, and violence. Cities once teeming with life became graveyards, silent and still.

A quarter of the earth's population withered away, their lives claimed by Death, while Hades swallowed their souls, pulling them into the abyss. The stench of decay hung heavy in the air, invisible but suffocating, as the world groaned under the crushing weight of the pale rider's passing.

And yet, the worst was still to come.

The scroll remained in the Lamb's hand, and when the fourth rider had completed his mission, the Lamb moved to the next seal. There was no pause, no respite for the earth, as the fifth seal was broken. This time, the heavens themselves seemed to still, holding their breath in reverence. The scene shifted from the devastation below to something higher, holier—a place where time had no meaning.

Beneath the altar in heaven, the souls of those who had been slain for their testimony, for the Word of God, cried out as one voice. Their bodies had long since perished, their blood spilled on the earth, but their souls burned bright, filled with an unwavering light that could never be extinguished. These were the martyrs, the ones who had suffered, who had endured through persecution and death, their faith carrying them to this place, waiting for justice.

"How long, O Lord, holy and true," they cried, "dost thou not judge and avenge our blood on them that dwell on the earth?"

Their voices rose in unison, filled with longing—not for vengeance out of hate, but for justice, for the righteousness of God to be fulfilled on the earth. They had watched as those who had condemned them continued to walk free, unpunished for their cruelty, and now, they called out for the Lord to act. They had suffered, and still, more would suffer in the days to come. The time for judgment had not yet reached its fullness, but the martyrs felt it approaching, their anticipation building with each cry.

In response, a voice thundered from the throne, and white robes were given to each of them. The robes were a sign of their victory, their purity in the eyes of the Lord. They had endured the greatest trials of faith, had stood firm even unto death, and now they were clothed in righteousness. But even in their triumph, they were told to rest.

"Rest yet for a little season," the voice said, gentle but firm, "until your fellow servants and your brethren, who will also be killed as you were, should be fulfilled."

The martyrs, though eager for the final judgment, understood. The suffering was not yet complete. More of their brothers and sisters would face the sword, the noose, the fire. The persecution would continue, and the blood of the faithful would stain the earth once more. But the end was coming. It was written in the scroll, and soon the seals would be finished.

As they rested beneath the altar, clothed in their robes of white, their voices quieted, though their hearts still burned with hope. The world below continued to suffer, to groan beneath the weight of the seals that had been broken. But even as death swept across the earth, and the souls of the martyrs cried for justice, a greater purpose moved beneath it all.

The pale horse still roamed the earth, and Death claimed his victims, while Hades opened wide to swallow those who had not known salvation. But in the heavens, the faithful waited, knowing that their God had not forgotten them, and that in the end, His justice would reign.

The fifth seal had revealed the suffering of the saints, and with it, the knowledge that even in death, their voices would not be silenced.

11

Seeking Shelter

Caleb's feet pounded the pavement, his breath coming in ragged bursts as he navigated the maze of alleyways and side streets. His heart raced, not just from exertion but from the fear that had been gnawing at his insides for days now, growing larger with every news update, every face he passed on the street. He couldn't remember the last time he'd felt calm, or even just...normal.

The city he once knew felt foreign to him now. It was like someone had taken the place he'd lived all his life and twisted it into something unrecognizable. Streets he had walked without a second thought were now filled with uncertainty. People moved with their heads down, arms clenched around whatever bags or boxes they had managed to gather. The grocery stores were either closed or overrun, shelves stripped bare, the aisles left in chaos. No one made eye contact anymore. The sense of community he had once taken for granted had vanished, replaced by a quiet, simmering panic that hung in the air like smoke.

He slowed as he neared the small apartment complex he had been heading toward, his eyes scanning the windows, looking for the faint glow of a light behind the curtains. His hand instinctively went to his pocket, feeling for the keycard he hadn't used in weeks. The weight of it, cool and heavy in his hand, felt strangely out of place—like a relic from a life that didn't belong to him anymore.

"Come on, Derek," Caleb muttered under his breath as he approached the building's front door. He buzzed the intercom, tapping his foot impatiently as he waited for a response. His pulse thrummed in his ears, and with each passing second, the cold knot of dread in his chest tightened.

The door clicked open, and Caleb slipped inside, grateful for the brief reprieve from the cold wind that had been biting at his face. The dimly lit hallway stretched out before him, and he hurried to the far end, his footsteps echoing off the tiled floor.

Derek stood in the doorway of his apartment, his face pale, eyes hollowed with the weight of sleepless nights. Caleb had seen the same look on everyone's faces lately—exhaustion mixed with a kind of desperate determination, like they were all holding onto some thin thread of hope that was fraying by the minute.

"Caleb," Derek said, his voice strained as he stepped aside to let him in. "You came."

"Yeah," Caleb said, glancing around the cramped apartment. It looked worse than the last time he'd been here. Half-empty bottles of water were scattered across the counter, and the small table by the window was littered with cans of food, most of them opened but barely touched. It was the kind of mess that spoke of people too worn down to care anymore.

"You need help," Caleb said, cutting straight to the point. "What's going on?"

Derek sighed, running a hand through his hair. He looked older, more worn down than the last time Caleb had seen him—like he'd aged ten years in just a few days. "It's bad, Caleb. Worse than what they're showing on the news."

Caleb swallowed hard, his mouth suddenly dry. "What do you mean? What's happening?"

Derek gestured for him to sit, but Caleb stayed on his feet, too restless to settle. He could feel the tension in the room, the heaviness that had been growing since he'd walked in.

"They're not telling us everything," Derek said, his voice low, like he was afraid someone might overhear. "I went to the store yesterday, just to see if I could get something—anything. There was nothing left. I mean, the shelves were cleared out. People were fighting over scraps, literally ripping food out of each other's hands."

Caleb shook his head, trying to wrap his mind around it. "It can't be that bad everywhere. There's got to be something the government is doing, right? Emergency supplies, shelters... something?"

Derek's laugh was bitter, a short, hollow sound. "There's nothing, man. Nothing we can rely on. People are scared. They're not just panicking—they're desperate. And when people get desperate, they start doing things they wouldn't normally do."

Caleb's stomach twisted, the knot of dread tightening even more. He'd known things were bad, but hearing Derek say it out loud made it feel real in a way that all the headlines and news reports hadn't.

"What about you?" Derek asked, leaning back against the counter, arms crossed. "You look like you've been through hell too."

Caleb let out a shaky breath, running his hands over his face. "I don't know, man. It feels like everything's falling apart. My sister's gone." His voice cracked as he said it, the weight of the words still fresh and heavy. "She didn't even make it through the week. She starved before they could do anything for her."

Derek's face softened, and for a moment, the tension in the room eased. "I'm sorry, Caleb. I didn't know."

Caleb shook his head, swallowing the lump in his throat. "It's not just her. It's everywhere. People are dying—starving, sick, fighting in the streets. I don't even recognize this city anymore."

For a long moment, they stood in silence, the reality of what they were facing pressing down on them like an unbearable weight. Caleb could feel the world shifting beneath his feet, the certainty he had once held onto slipping away. He had always been the guy who believed in reason, in the ability of people to figure things out, to fix whatever was broken. But now, as he looked at the empty shelves, the darkened streets, the faces of people who had given up hope, he wasn't so sure anymore.

Derek shifted, his gaze darting toward the window. "I don't know how much longer we can last like this. The food's almost gone. We're rationing what we have left, but... it's not enough."

Caleb wanted to say something reassuring, wanted to offer some solution, but he couldn't. He didn't have answers. No one did. He felt like they were all just trying to stay afloat in a world that was sinking faster than they could swim.

"I thought I could make it through this," Caleb said, his voice low. "I thought I could figure it out, you know? But... now I don't know. I don't know if we're going to make it."

Derek didn't answer, but his silence said everything. They were both thinking it, even if neither of them wanted to say it out loud.

The world was collapsing, and there was nothing they could do to stop it.

Caleb felt his phone buzz in his pocket, breaking the heavy silence. He pulled it out, glancing at the screen. It was Rachel. Again. He stared at the message she'd sent, the same kind of thing she'd been saying for weeks now—something about trusting in God, about finding peace in faith. He hadn't replied, not to this one or the dozen others she'd sent. He didn't have the energy to argue with her. And he didn't have the patience to hear any more talk about faith when the world was crumbling around him.

He shoved the phone back into his pocket, his chest tightening with the familiar frustration. Rachel didn't get it. She didn't understand what it was like out here, what it felt like to watch everything you believed in fall apart.

Derek must have noticed the look on his face because he spoke up, his voice quieter this time. "You've been talking to her, haven't you? Rachel?"

Caleb shrugged, avoiding Derek's gaze. "She's been sending me messages. Telling me to trust God or something."

Derek let out a long breath, his eyes heavy with understanding. "Maybe she's got a point."

Caleb's jaw clenched, the anger rising in him before he could stop it. "What, you think some prayer is going to fix this? You think faith is going to make food appear out of thin air?"

Derek didn't respond right away, but when he did, his voice was calm, steady. "I don't know, man. But it might give us something to hold on to. And right now, I think that's the only thing we've got left."

Caleb didn't answer. He couldn't. Instead, he stood there, feeling the weight of Derek's words settle over him like a lead blanket, pressing down on him, making it hard to breathe. The world outside was burning, and inside, everything felt like it was falling apart.

12

The Persecution Begins

Rachel knelt in the shadowed corner of her living room, the soft glow of a single candle casting flickering shapes across the walls. Her Bible lay open on the floor before her, the familiar verses shining faintly under the soft light, but her eyes were closed, her hands folded tightly in prayer.

The quiet of her apartment felt like a blessing in these days when the noise of the world outside grew louder, more hostile with every passing hour. The chaos had reached a fever pitch—food riots, the desperate looting of stores, and even more disturbing whispers of believers being rounded up in cities far from here. Rachel had always known it was coming, had read about it in scripture, but the reality of it still pressed on her chest, a weight she couldn't shake.

"Father," she whispered, her voice barely audible above the steady hum of her breath, "we need You now more than ever. Strengthen us, Lord. Strengthen Your people to endure what's to come."

She exhaled slowly, the prayer grounding her, as it always did. In these last few weeks, the world had grown darker, but her faith had grown brighter—like a small, steady flame that refused to be snuffed out. The words of the Bible had never felt more alive, more real. She could see the truth of it unfolding before her eyes, and though fear gnawed at the edges of her heart, she felt a sense of peace. A peace that only faith could bring.

A sharp knock on the door broke her concentration, sending her heart racing. Rachel froze, her hands stilling over her Bible. She wasn't expecting anyone—especially not this late. The knocking came again, more urgent this time. Whoever was on the other side wasn't going to wait much longer.

She rose to her feet, moving quickly but cautiously, and peered through the peephole. It was Sarah. Relief flooded Rachel's chest, but the expression on Sarah's face—a mixture of fear and panic—sent a jolt of unease down her spine.

Rachel unlocked the door, pulling it open just wide enough to let Sarah slip inside. Her friend stumbled in, her breath ragged, eyes wide and wild.

"They came for them," Sarah gasped, her voice trembling. "They came for the Johnsons."

Rachel shut the door behind her, her own heart pounding now. "Who? Who came for them?"

"The police. Or...I don't know, it wasn't normal police. They didn't have badges, just uniforms. Black vans. They came in the middle of the night. The whole family's gone. I saw it happen. They didn't even fight back."

Rachel felt her stomach drop. The Johnson family had been pillars in the church for years—faithful, kind, always the first to help anyone in need. They were the type of people who everyone trusted. And now they were gone.

She swallowed hard, her mind racing. This was what she had been preparing for, what she had prayed about, but now that it was here, it felt surreal. Persecution had always been something that happened far away—other countries, other times. Not here. Not in her town.

"Why?" Rachel asked softly, though she already knew the answer.

Sarah's eyes filled with tears as she sank into the worn armchair near the window. "I don't know. I just know they're taking believers. People who... people who won't stop talking about God. It's starting, Rachel. It's really starting."

Rachel stood still for a moment, the weight of Sarah's words pressing down on her. She had known this was coming. The warnings had been in scripture, clear and unyielding, but now that it was here, now that she was standing in the middle of it, it felt like a punch to the gut.

She took a deep breath and crossed the room, kneeling down beside Sarah, placing a comforting hand on her knee. "I know it's hard. It's terrifying. But we knew this was coming, didn't we? Jesus told us this would happen. *'Then shall they deliver you up to be afflicted, and shall kill you: and ye shall be hated of all nations for my name's sake.'*"

Sarah shook her head, her tears spilling over. "I didn't think it would be like this. I didn't think it would be so fast. They're just...gone. No trial, no warning, nothing. They were praying, and now they're gone."

Rachel squeezed Sarah's hand, her own heart aching, but her resolve was stronger than ever. "It's going to get worse before it gets better, Sarah. But we're not alone. God's with us, even in this. *Especially* in this."

Sarah's lips quivered, her eyes searching Rachel's face for the reassurance she needed. "What are we going to do? What if they come for us next?"

Rachel's throat tightened, but she didn't flinch. "Then we keep our faith. We keep praying, we keep standing firm in what we believe. This world isn't our home. It never was."

She let her words settle, hoping they would sink into Sarah's heart the way they had settled into her own weeks ago, when she had first realized the full weight of what was happening. The persecution wasn't just coming—it had arrived. And it wouldn't stop with the Johnsons.

"I can't go back home," Sarah whispered, her hands trembling. "What if they come to my place next?"

"You can stay here," Rachel offered immediately. "At least for tonight. We'll figure things out in the morning."

Sarah nodded weakly, wiping at her tear-streaked face. "I don't know what to do, Rachel. I feel like I'm falling apart. I keep praying, but... I'm so scared."

Rachel leaned closer, her voice soft but steady. "I'm scared too, Sarah. But God didn't promise that we wouldn't face persecution. He promised that He would be with us through it. We have to hold on to that. He's here, even when it feels like everything is falling apart."

The sound of distant sirens cut through the quiet of the apartment, and Rachel's pulse quickened. The sirens had become more frequent in recent days, always a reminder of how quickly the world outside was spiraling. She didn't know who the next target would be, but she knew one thing for sure: it wouldn't stop with just one family.

"Come on," Rachel said, standing and pulling Sarah up with her. "We're going to pray."

Sarah hesitated for a moment, her face pale, but she followed Rachel to the corner of the room, where they both knelt. The candlelight flickered as they bowed their heads, the faint hum of the city outside blending with the sound of their whispered prayers.

Rachel's voice was steady as she began, her words pouring out with quiet conviction. "Father, we need You now more than ever. We know You see what's happening. You see the fear in our hearts, and You see the evil that's taking hold of the world around us. But we trust You. We trust that You're in control, that You will strengthen us to endure, no matter what comes. Give us courage, Lord. Give us peace in the midst of this storm."

Sarah's voice joined hers, shaky at first, but growing stronger with each word. They prayed for protection, for wisdom, for the strength to stand firm in their faith, even as the walls of the world closed in around them.

And as they prayed, Rachel felt it again—that quiet, unshakable peace. It settled over her like a blanket, soft and warm, reminding her that no matter what came next, she wasn't alone. God was with her. He always had been, and He always would be.

The persecution had begun. But so had the endurance of the saints.

13

The Sixth Seal

Revelation 6:12-17

Far above the earth, the scroll trembled once more in the Lamb's hand. With a movement as subtle as a breath, the sixth seal was opened. The sound of its breaking did not echo like thunder or crash through the heavens in a wave, but the impact of it rippled through the very fabric of existence, felt not just by the earth but by the stars, the skies, and all of creation.

The earth groaned as if wounded, and the heavens began to unravel.

It started with the ground—a low, deep rumbling that spread beneath the surface of the earth like a great beast stirring from its slumber. Across every continent, in cities and countrysides alike, the tremors began to rise. Buildings shuddered, their foundations cracking and shifting. The streets buckled, sidewalks splitting open as if the earth itself was being torn apart. The first wave of quakes hit suddenly, violently, as though the world had been thrust into the throes of a cosmic upheaval.

The skies, once calm and clear, began to change. The sun, high in the sky, dimmed, its light flickering like a dying flame. Slowly, agonizingly, the once-brilliant orb darkened until it was nothing more than a cold, black disc hanging in the sky, casting a deep, unnatural shadow over the earth. Where there had once been warmth and light, there was now only a suffocating, oppressive darkness.

People looked up in disbelief, their faces pale in the eerie half-light. The sun—something so constant, so immovable—was gone. Panic rippled through the crowds as they stared at the sky, at the growing shadows that stretched across the land. It was as if time itself had faltered, as though the world had been plunged into some forgotten era, a time before light had been spoken into being.

Then, the moon rose, but it was not the cool, silver sphere that had guided the night sky for millennia. It climbed the horizon slowly, almost reluctantly, and as it did, the world saw that it had turned the color of blood. Deep, crimson red, as though the very essence of life had been drained from the earth and cast into the heavens. It hung there, casting a dim, unnatural glow over the darkened land, staining the faces of those who looked up in fear.

People began to scream.

In cities and towns, in the sprawling wilderness and along the coasts, the collective cry of humanity rose as one, piercing the unnatural silence. Mothers clutched their children to their chests, their eyes wide with terror. Men fell to their knees, their hands trembling as they reached out to the empty air, as though begging for the world to right itself. Priests, ministers, and pastors raised their arms toward the sky, praying aloud, their voices trembling as they called upon God to bring mercy, to make the heavens clear once more.

But mercy did not come.

As the earth continued to tremble and the sky darkened, a new horror emerged. The stars—once steady and fixed, the celestial map that had guided sailors, travelers, and dreamers for centuries—began to fall. One by one, like sparks shaken from a dying flame, they plunged from the sky, streaking across the darkness like fiery arrows loosed from an unseen bow. They fell with a terrifying brilliance, leaving trails of light in their wake as they descended toward the earth.

Each star that fell brought with it a great wind, a rush of air that tore through the cities and villages, flattening trees, toppling buildings, and sending debris flying. The stars struck the earth with devastating force, igniting fires, splitting the land, and sending shockwaves across the globe. The very sky seemed to be collapsing in on itself, as if the heavens were being rolled back like a scroll, exposing the raw, chaotic force of the universe behind it.

The panic that had begun with the sun and the moon now reached a fever pitch. In every corner of the world, people fled in every direction, seeking shelter, seeking safety, but there was none to be found. The earth quaked beneath their feet, the stars fell from above, and the air was thick with the smoke of fires ignited by the celestial destruction.

In the great cities, the rich and powerful, those who had once thought themselves immune to the trials of the world, now cowered in fear. Kings, presidents, the wealthy elite—they fled from their palaces, their towers, and their mansions, seeking refuge in caves and mountainsides, begging the earth to hide them from the wrath that had descended upon them.

"Fall on us!" they cried, their voices ragged with fear. "Hide us from the face of Him that sits on the throne, and from the wrath of the Lamb! For the great day of His wrath has come, and who can stand?"

They had seen the truth now, seen it written in the sky, in the stars, and in the trembling earth beneath their feet. What they had once dismissed as myth, as superstition, had now become a terrifying reality. The natural world itself was unraveling, and with it, their carefully constructed lives, their power, their wealth—none of it mattered anymore.

Across the world, the recognition spread like wildfire. Something supernatural, something far beyond human control or comprehension, had begun. This was not just a disaster, not just a catastrophic event brought on by the whims of nature. This was judgment. The world was being shaken, not by the forces of the earth, but by the hand of God.

And as the heavens continued to collapse, as the stars fell and the earth quaked, the world collectively trembled. They had no answers, no recourse, no shelter from what was coming. All they could do was wait—wait and fear—because the end, it seemed, was no longer something they could ignore. It was here. And no one, not the powerful or the meek, could escape its reach.

The sixth seal had been broken, and the earth, the sky, and all of creation cried out in response.

14

A World in Chaos

Caleb stood frozen in the middle of the street, his breath catching in his throat as the ground beneath him shuddered violently. The buildings around him trembled, windows rattling in their frames, the rumbling of the earth like a living, growling beast beneath his feet. He braced himself against a streetlight, trying to steady his legs as the quake rolled through the city, a wave of destruction that seemed to have no end.

A deep, unsettling crack echoed from somewhere nearby, followed by the groaning collapse of concrete and steel. People screamed. A thick cloud of dust billowed up from the intersection ahead, swallowing everything in its path. Caleb's heart pounded in his chest, his lungs burning with every shallow breath he managed to suck in.

Around him, chaos had erupted. The crowd that had gathered earlier—protesters, bystanders, people just trying to make it through another day—now scattered in every direction, their faces twisted in fear. Cars screeched to a halt, horns blaring as drivers abandoned their vehicles in the middle of the street. Some people sprinted toward buildings, hoping for shelter, while others knelt where they stood, their hands over their heads as if that alone could protect them from what was happening.

"Run!" someone shouted from the crowd, their voice barely audible over the deafening roar of the earth and the panicked cries of those around them.

But Caleb couldn't move. His feet felt cemented to the pavement, his body paralyzed by the sheer enormity of what was unfolding. This wasn't just a protest gone wrong or another riot. This was something else, something he had never imagined. The city—his city—was breaking apart right in front of him.

A woman stumbled past him, clutching a small child to her chest, her face streaked with tears and dirt. She barely looked at him as she passed, her focus entirely on keeping her balance, on keeping moving. Caleb's eyes followed her, but the movement around him blurred, his mind struggling to make sense of the scene.

He looked up, the sky darkening above him. The sun, which had been barely visible through the haze of city pollution just hours ago, had transformed into a black void, its light completely extinguished. The air felt thick and oppressive, the sudden loss of daylight casting everything in a strange, unnatural twilight. And then, above the trembling earth, the moon appeared—a dull, menacing red, as if it had been drenched in blood. It hung low in the sky, casting an eerie glow over the chaos below.

Caleb stared up at it, his mouth dry. He had heard about eclipses before, had even seen one as a kid. But this—this was different. There was something wrong about the way the moon looked, something that sent a chill crawling up his spine. The blood-red light bathed the crumbling city in an otherworldly hue, turning the chaos into something nightmarish.

A tremor rippled through the ground again, this one stronger than the last. Caleb stumbled, his hand slipping from the streetlight as he fell to his knees. The concrete beneath him cracked, fissures snaking across the street, splitting open the pavement like a shattered mirror. The sound of collapsing buildings filled the air, dust and debris rising into the sky like smoke.

For a brief moment, the shaking stopped. Caleb lifted his head, his chest heaving as he tried to catch his breath. The streets, once filled with the noise of life, now lay in eerie silence. People had stopped running. They stood frozen, eyes wide with disbelief as they looked toward the heavens.

And then the stars began to fall.

At first, it was just a single streak of light—a bright, glowing trail that shot across the darkened sky. Then another. And another. Soon, the sky was alive with falling stars, each one cutting through the air with a blinding flash before disappearing beyond the horizon or crashing into the earth. Caleb watched, mesmerized, as the stars streaked down like flaming arrows, their fiery trails lighting up the blood-red moon.

The ground beneath him rumbled again, but he barely noticed. His mind couldn't process what he was seeing. Stars weren't supposed to fall like this, not in such numbers, not with such intensity. It was like the sky itself was being torn apart, the very fabric of the universe unraveling in front of him.

A bright flash of light erupted from somewhere nearby, followed by a deafening boom. Caleb flinched, throwing his arms over his head as a shockwave of heat and dust blasted through the street. He could hear glass shattering, metal groaning as it twisted under the force. Another building had collapsed, but he couldn't bring himself to look.

Panic rose in his throat, his heart hammering against his ribcage. He wanted to scream, to shout, to run, but his body wouldn't respond. The sky was falling, the earth was breaking, and he was just...stuck.

His phone buzzed in his pocket, the vibration barely noticeable in the chaos. With shaking hands, he pulled it out, the screen lighting up with a text. It was from Rachel.

> **Rachel:** *Caleb, please. Are you okay? I'm praying for you. This is what I was telling you about. Please listen now.*

He stared at the words, his chest tightening. Rachel had been talking about this for weeks, about the signs, about the world coming apart at the seams. She had begged him to listen, but he hadn't. He hadn't believed any of it—until now.

A loud crash brought him back to the present, the sound of metal grinding against metal as another streetlamp fell, crashing into the ground just feet from where he knelt. The sparks from the fallen wires lit up the darkness, casting brief, jagged shadows across the pavement.

Caleb scrambled to his feet, his legs shaking as he turned, his eyes searching for some kind of escape. The crowd had scattered in every direction, and the streets around him were littered with debris. Cars were overturned, their windows shattered. Buildings that had once stood tall were now crumbling, some of them reduced to nothing more than piles of rubble.

The stars kept falling, one after the other, streaking across the sky like fiery rain. The heat from the explosions hung in the air, mixed with the choking dust of collapsed structures.

As he staggered forward, his feet crunching over broken glass, the words from Rachel's text echoed in his mind. *This is what I was telling you about.* He hadn't believed her then, but now... now, with the sky falling and the ground shaking, he wasn't sure what to believe.

He looked up again, his eyes drawn to the blood-red moon, and for the first time in his life, Caleb felt something he had never expected to feel.

Fear.

Not the fear of losing his job, or missing a bill payment, or even of dying. This was something deeper, something that gripped his soul in a way that left him trembling.

This was fear of something greater, something beyond him—something that couldn't be explained away by science or logic. Something that felt, inescapably, like judgment.

The ground shook again, but this time, Caleb didn't fall. He stood there, staring at the sky, the realization sinking in like a weight in his chest.

The world was ending.

15

A Time for Prayer

Rachel sat on the floor of her living room, the dim light of a single candle flickering in front of her. The room was silent except for the steady rhythm of her breathing. Her Bible lay open on her lap, her fingers brushing lightly over the pages as she traced the familiar verses. The weight of everything pressed down on her, but in this moment, she felt calm—centered in the only place that still made sense.

The sun had turned black hours ago. She had watched in awe and dread as the daylight disappeared, leaving the world cast in a shadow that felt both ominous and holy. Now, the only light came from the red moon outside, its eerie glow seeping through the edges of the drawn curtains. The blood-colored light stained the room in shades of crimson, but Rachel kept her focus on the words in front of her, letting them ground her.

Her heart was heavy, not just with the fear of what was happening around her, but with the certainty of what was coming next. She had always known that the end times would be terrifying, that the world would be shaken to its core. She had read it over and over again, prayed about it, prepared for it in her heart. But knowing and experiencing it were two different things.

The tremors had been the first sign. She had felt them hours ago, the ground trembling beneath her feet, rattling the windows and shaking the furniture. Then came the darkness, sudden and unnatural, casting the world into a twilight that seemed to suffocate the air. Now, the stars were falling, streaking across the sky like fiery arrows, and with each one, Rachel could feel the world inching closer to its breaking point.

Her phone vibrated softly next to her Bible, and she reached for it, glancing at the screen. Another text from Sarah.

> **Sarah:** *I'm scared. I don't know what to do. The sky is falling, Rach. What do we do?*

Rachel closed her eyes for a moment, breathing deeply, letting the tension in her chest settle. She understood Sarah's fear. She felt it too. But she couldn't let it consume her—not now. Not when everything was unraveling so quickly.

She texted back quickly, her fingers steady.

> **Rachel:** *Pray, Sarah. Now is the time to pray. Trust in God's promises. He's with us through all of this.*

She set the phone aside and let her gaze fall on the candle's flame, small and fragile in the vast darkness. The words of the Bible echoed in her mind, familiar verses about faith in the face of fear, about trusting in the Lord when the world was falling apart.

> *"God is our refuge and strength, a very present help in trouble. Therefore will not we fear, though the earth be removed, and though the mountains be carried into the midst of the sea."*

The ground shook again beneath her, and she steadied herself with a hand on the floor, her heart skipping a beat at the force of the tremor. Outside, she could hear the faint sounds of panic—sirens wailing in the distance, the muted shouts of neighbors as they gathered in confusion and fear. The world was breaking, just as it had been foretold.

Rachel knelt on the floor, her hands clasped in front of her, head bowed as she whispered the only words that came to her in that moment.

"Father, be with us. Be with Your people. Strengthen us for what's to come. Give us courage. Give us peace. We trust You, even now, as the world trembles around us."

Her voice wavered slightly, but she pressed on, each word lifting her spirit a little higher, bringing her closer to the peace she knew could only come from God. The fear was still there, lingering at the edges of her thoughts, but it no longer held power over her.

Another tremor rocked the ground, this one stronger than the last. The candle flickered violently, the light threatening to extinguish itself before settling once again into a steady flame. Rachel's pulse quickened, but her resolve remained unshaken.

She reached for her Bible once more, her eyes scanning the pages for comfort, for answers. She found them in the familiar verses of Matthew 24, the words that had warned her of these days long ago.

> *"Immediately after the tribulation of those days shall the sun be darkened, and the moon shall not give her light, and the stars shall fall from heaven, and the powers of the heavens shall be shaken."*

It was happening. Every word, every prophecy—it was happening right before her eyes.

Rachel stood and moved to the window, parting the curtains just enough to see the sky. The moon, blood-red and low in the sky, loomed like a terrible omen over the city. Stars continued to fall, streaking across the sky in fiery arcs, their brilliance illuminating the dark streets below.

She could see her neighbors, huddled together in small groups, their faces pale with terror. Some were crying, others were shouting, their voices carrying faintly through the window. A few had fallen to their knees, their hands clasped in desperate prayer, while others stood frozen, staring up at the sky in disbelief.

Rachel closed her eyes, the weight of the moment pressing down on her. She could feel it—the fear, the confusion, the overwhelming sense of loss that radiated from the people outside. The world was falling apart, and they didn't know where to turn, didn't know how to make sense of what was happening.

But Rachel did.

"God, help them see," she whispered, her breath fogging the glass as she spoke. "Help them see that You're still here, that You haven't abandoned us."

The weight of her prayer lingered in the air, heavy with the unspoken plea that so many others were likely lifting up in the darkness. Rachel knew that not everyone would understand, that not everyone would turn to God in these final days. But she prayed for them anyway, because that's what she had been called to do.

The room shook again, a heavy vibration that rattled the furniture and sent the candle's flame dancing wildly. The ground was growing more unstable, the tremors more frequent. It wouldn't be long now before the world as she knew it was completely undone.

Rachel stepped back from the window, her mind settling into a calm, focused clarity. She knew what she had to do. There was no stopping what was happening, no reversing the course that had been set in motion. But she could pray. She could hold fast to the faith that had carried her through every storm in her life, and she could trust in the God who had promised to never leave her.

She returned to the floor, her knees pressing into the soft rug as she closed her eyes and bowed her head. The sounds of the collapsing world faded into the background, replaced by the steady rhythm of her heartbeat, by the quiet strength of her faith.

"Lord," she whispered, her voice soft but unwavering, "I will not be afraid. I will trust in You, even now. Even as the stars fall and the earth shakes, I will trust in You."

The candle flickered, casting long, dancing shadows across the room. But the flame did not go out.

And neither would her faith.

16

Unbearable Fear

Caleb sat in the dim light of his apartment, the curtains drawn tightly over the windows, shutting out the world outside. His phone buzzed on the table beside him, but he didn't reach for it. It had been ringing off and on for days—friends, coworkers, maybe even his mom, trying to get through to him—but he couldn't bring himself to answer. The world outside was unraveling, and he didn't have anything to say.

The silence was thick, unnatural. It settled into the corners of the room like fog, clinging to him, making the air feel heavy. There had been moments in the past few days where everything seemed to just... stop. The constant rumble of the earth had faded, the noise of panic in the streets quieted, even the sky, once lit by the eerie glow of the red moon, had gone black, like someone had flipped a switch. It was as if the whole world was waiting—holding its breath, waiting for something terrible to happen.

Caleb sat with his head in his hands, his thoughts a swirling mess of confusion, fear, and frustration. It didn't make sense. None of it made sense. The tremors, the blood-red moon, the stars falling from the sky—it was like something out of a nightmare. And yet, here he was, living it. The things he had brushed off as superstition, the things Rachel had tried to warn him about—it all seemed to be happening.

But he couldn't—*wouldn't*—believe that.

He ran his hands through his hair, tugging at the strands as if the pressure might somehow keep his thoughts from spiraling out of control. There had to be an explanation for this. A scientific reason. Some kind of rational, logical answer. He just didn't know what it was yet.

A cold sweat clung to his skin, his body trembling with an unease he couldn't shake. He hadn't left the apartment in days. Maybe more. Time had become a blur, one long stretch of suffocating silence and anxiety. The news had stopped broadcasting regularly—power outages were spreading, and communication lines were failing. The few snippets of information he managed to get were more confusing than helpful. People were talking about the "chosen ones" now—rumors of people being marked, protected from what was coming next.

He scoffed at the thought, though there was no one to hear him. *Chosen ones*. It was just another rumor. Another wild theory to explain what couldn't be explained. Superstition. Fear breeding more fear.

But still, the idea gnawed at the edges of his mind. What if there was something to it? What if Rachel had been right all along? She had talked about this—about signs, about the end times, about things that were coming that he couldn't begin to comprehend. She had tried to warn him, pleaded with him to listen. He had dismissed her, waved it off as religious nonsense.

Now, he wasn't so sure.

Caleb pushed himself up from the couch and began pacing the small space, his hands clenched into fists at his sides. His heart pounded in his chest, faster than it should have been. He hadn't slept in days, not really. Every time he closed his eyes, he saw it—the stars falling from the sky like fire, the moon glowing blood-red, the earth splitting open beneath his feet.

He glanced toward the window, hesitating. Part of him wanted to look, to pull the curtains back and see what was happening out there. But the other part—the larger part—couldn't face it. Whatever was out there, he wasn't ready to see it.

His phone buzzed again, and this time, he snatched it off the table, gripping it tightly in his hand as he read the message that had just come through.

Rachel: *Caleb, I'm praying for you. I know you don't believe me, but please, just listen. God is still waiting for you. It's not too late.*

He stared at the words, his jaw clenching. She still thought she could save him. She still believed that he could just *choose* to have faith and everything would somehow be okay. That's what Rachel didn't understand. He couldn't just... believe. It wasn't in him. He had spent his entire life grounded in reality, in the tangible, in what he could see and hear and touch. Faith? God? That wasn't something he could grasp.

And yet...

The silence pressed in around him, the stillness so thick it felt like a living thing, wrapping itself around his throat, making it hard to breathe. The longer it went on, the more it felt like something was coming—something huge, something unavoidable. The calm before the storm. He had always heard that phrase, but now, for the first time, he *felt* it. The world was holding its breath, waiting for the next disaster to strike, and Caleb didn't know if he could handle it.

A sharp knock on the door jolted him out of his thoughts. He froze, his heart racing. He hadn't seen anyone in days. Who would be knocking now?

For a long moment, he didn't move. The knock came again, more insistent this time. Caleb swallowed, his mouth dry, and slowly made his way to the door. His hand hovered over the doorknob, hesitation holding him back.

"Caleb?" a voice called from the other side, muffled but familiar.

Rachel.

His pulse quickened, a mixture of relief and frustration flooding through him. Of course, it was Rachel. She had probably come to check on him, to drag him out of his isolation and force him to listen to another one of her sermons about faith.

Caleb unlocked the door and pulled it open, and there she stood, her face pale, her eyes filled with that same quiet determination she always had when she talked about God. She stepped inside without waiting for an invitation, her hands folded in front of her.

"You haven't been answering my texts," she said softly, her eyes scanning the room, taking in the state of his apartment—the clutter, the empty bottles, the unmade couch that had become his bed.

"I'm fine," Caleb muttered, though even he could hear the lie in his voice.

Rachel raised an eyebrow, but she didn't push him. Instead, she stepped closer, her expression softening. "I'm worried about you."

Caleb ran a hand through his hair, pacing again. "There's nothing to worry about. I'm just... trying to figure things out. Like everyone else."

"Like everyone else?" Rachel's voice was gentle but firm. "Caleb, you've locked yourself away in here. You can't keep hiding. The world is changing, and I know you see it. I know you *feel* it."

He stopped pacing and turned to face her, his frustration bubbling to the surface. "What do you want me to say, Rachel? That you were right? That this is all some kind of divine punishment? That God's real and I'm just too stubborn to see it?"

Rachel's eyes didn't waver. She stepped closer, her voice quiet. "I just want you to open your heart. I'm not asking you to figure it all out right now. I'm asking you to trust that maybe, just maybe, there's more to this than what you can see."

Caleb looked away, his chest tightening. The silence pressed in again, suffocating him. He wanted to believe her—wanted to believe that there was something beyond all of this chaos, something bigger than the fear gnawing at him. But he couldn't. He didn't know how.

"I can't," he whispered, his voice cracking.

Rachel reached out and touched his arm, her grip gentle but strong. "You can. It's not too late. But you have to choose."

Caleb shook his head, pulling away from her touch. The fear was unbearable, twisting in his gut, clawing at his mind. He couldn't let go of it, couldn't make sense of the world anymore, and yet... he was afraid of what might happen if he tried to believe.

The silence lingered between them, heavy with unspoken words, and in that silence, Caleb felt the storm coming.

And he didn't know if he was strong enough to face it.

17

THE BEGINNING OF THE END

Caleb stood in the middle of what used to be a bustling city street, but now, it was something else entirely. The world around him had become a nightmare, a hellscape of chaos and destruction that seemed to swallow everything whole. He could barely recognize the place where he had spent his entire life. Skyscrapers once towering and confident now lay in heaps of rubble, their skeletons twisted and blackened by fire. The acrid smell of smoke clung to the air, choking him with every breath, and the sky above was dark—far too dark for the middle of the day.

The sun... It had been there just hours ago, weak and pale, as if struggling to keep its light alive. Now, it was almost gone, hidden behind a blanket of darkness that stretched across the horizon. The cold that followed was biting, unnatural, sending shivers through him even though his heart pounded with a kind of fevered panic. It felt like the end of everything. Not just of his city, or his country, but of the world itself. Civilization, as he had known it, was crumbling into dust, and there was nothing anyone could do to stop it.

His mind raced, desperate for answers. There had to be something—a scientific explanation for what was happening. There always was. But nothing made sense anymore. Firestorms had swept through the city earlier in the day, appearing as though from nowhere, setting buildings and cars ablaze without warning. People had screamed, their voices high-pitched with terror, running from the flames only to find themselves trapped between walls of fire and collapsed buildings. And then came the water.

The reports had started trickling in after the firestorms—people drinking from the city's water supply, only to collapse minutes later, writhing in pain, their lips turning blue. The river had turned an unnatural color, a deep, sickly green, and the lakes were no better. The poison spread quickly, and with it, the panic. Caleb had seen it with his own eyes—people fighting for bottled water in stores, smashing through glass doors and looting anything they could get their hands on. The desperation in their eyes was unlike anything he had ever witnessed.

He'd tried to get to the hospital, to see if anyone had an answer, if there was a way to purify the water or stop the madness that was unfolding. But when he got there, the building was overrun, chaos spilling into the streets. People flooded the emergency room, their bodies broken and bleeding from the tremors that had cracked the sidewalks and toppled streetlights. Others lay in beds, their skin ashen from the poison they had unknowingly consumed. Doctors and nurses moved through the crowd with hollow eyes, their faces a mask of exhaustion and hopelessness.

Caleb had stood there, in the middle of it all, feeling completely useless. He'd always been a man who trusted in reason, in science. But science wasn't giving him answers now. The medical teams had no cure, no way to purify the poisoned water. The fires couldn't be explained—there were no gas leaks, no electrical malfunctions. It was as though the earth itself had turned on them.

He remembered the way people had looked at the sky just before the sun had dimmed. Eyes wide, filled with horror as the light slowly faded, as the temperature dropped and the stars themselves seemed to vanish from view. It wasn't just a weather event. It wasn't something that could be explained by the natural order. Caleb had known it, even if he didn't want to admit it. This was something different. Something beyond him.

But he wasn't ready to give up. Not yet.

Stumbling through the debris-laden streets, Caleb pushed his way past the few stragglers who hadn't yet fled or given up. Some were huddled in alleyways, clutching what little food and water they had managed to hoard. Others sat in silence, their faces blank, staring into the distance as if the world no longer made sense to them. But Caleb couldn't stop. He had to find someone—anyone—who knew what was going on, who could help make sense of the collapse that was unraveling faster than he could process.

He glanced at his phone, its battery low, the screen flickering weakly. He had been trying to reach someone—anyone in authority. Emergency lines were down. There was no response from government agencies. Even the news stations had gone quiet. The few messages he had received were from people as lost as he was. Everyone was grasping at straws, trying to make sense of the carnage that surrounded them, but no one had any answers. Not even the scientists, the people he had trusted all his life to explain the unexplainable.

As he moved through the streets, his mind kept drifting back to the rumors he'd heard. Whispers about the "chosen ones," people who had been marked, sealed, protected from the devastation that was sweeping across the earth. He had scoffed at the idea when he first heard it—another superstition, another myth that desperate people clung to when they had nothing else. But now... now he wasn't so sure.

He could feel his resolve slipping, the edges of his disbelief crumbling under the weight of the horror around him. But still, he fought it. There *had* to be a rational explanation. There had to be something that made sense, that wasn't tied to prophecies or divine wrath. Humanity had always survived before. They had faced wars, famine, disease, and they had come out the other side. Surely they could do it again.

Caleb found himself in the center of a park, the once-green grass now charred and dead beneath his feet. The fountains, which had once been the gathering point for families, for children playing in the sun, were dry, cracked. He collapsed onto a bench, his chest heaving with exhaustion and dread. The cold air bit at his skin, and the unnatural darkness stretched out in all directions, making it feel as though the world had shrunk, that the horizon had closed in on itself.

His thoughts raced. He needed to find answers. Maybe there were scientists somewhere, maybe there was still a government, still leadership that could make sense of it all. Maybe humanity could claw its way back from this, even now, at the brink of total collapse.

But deep down, in the quiet parts of his mind that he refused to acknowledge, Caleb knew that science didn't have the answers anymore. He could see it in the chaos around him, in the way everything had unraveled so quickly, so completely. It wasn't just the earth breaking apart—it was the very fabric of existence. It was something bigger than humanity, something beyond their control.

Rachel's voice echoed in his mind, her words soft but persistent. *Caleb, I'm praying for you. It's not too late.*

He clenched his fists, his jaw tightening. He wasn't ready to surrender to that. Not yet.

But as the darkness deepened, as the fires continued to burn in the distance, as the poison seeped into the water and the sun remained dim, Caleb felt the walls closing in around him. His faith in humanity, in reason, was slipping away. And he was running out of places to turn.

The world was ending.

And he didn't know how much longer he could hold on.

18

WITNESSING THE WRATH

Rachel stood at her window, hands pressed against the cool glass as she watched the world outside unravel in slow, agonizing destruction. Flames rose in the distance, lighting up the darkened horizon in an eerie, orange glow. Smoke billowed upward, black and suffocating, blotting out the sky. She could barely make out the shapes of buildings, many of them crumbled, reduced to little more than rubble. It was like the earth itself was groaning under the weight of judgment, as if every corner of creation was being torn apart at the seams.

But Rachel's heart remained calm.

Her breath was steady, her mind quiet, even as the firestorms raged and the water turned to poison. She knew what she was seeing—*this* was the wrath of God, poured out over a world that had long rejected Him. The judgments that had been foretold, the ones she had read about and studied for years, were happening now, right before her eyes. It was terrifying and awe-inspiring at the same time, but it wasn't a surprise. Not to her. She had always known it would come to this.

The others—her neighbors, the people rushing through the streets in panic—hadn't known. They had lived their lives as if the world would keep spinning forever, oblivious to the warnings, blind to the signs. But Rachel had seen them, felt them deep in her soul. And now, as the earth shook and the sky darkened, she understood. This was the beginning of the end. And it was just.

She pulled her hands away from the window, turning to sit on the floor by her bed, where her Bible lay open. The room was dimly lit by the flickering of a candle, its soft light casting long shadows across the walls. She ran her fingers over the pages, her lips moving in silent prayer.

"Lord, Your will is being done," she whispered, her voice filled with reverence. "Your judgments are righteous, and Your justice is true. I pray for those who are suffering, those who are lost in this storm. Bring them to repentance, Lord. Open their hearts to see You, even now."

Rachel's hands trembled slightly as she closed her eyes, feeling the weight of the world's pain, but also the peace that came from knowing God was in control. She knew that this destruction wasn't random. It wasn't chaos for the sake of chaos. It was the consequence of centuries of rebellion, of humanity turning away from its Creator. She didn't take pleasure in the suffering—far from it. Her heart ached for those who hadn't yet seen the truth, for those who were still lost. But she also knew that this was necessary. It was all part of God's plan to bring the world back to Him.

She opened her Bible, her eyes scanning the familiar verses of Revelation, her mind quieting as the words of prophecy flowed through her.

> *"And the third angel sounded, and there fell a great star from heaven, burning as it were a lamp, and it fell upon the third part of the rivers, and upon the fountains of waters; and the name of the star is called Wormwood: and the third part of the waters became wormwood; and many men died of the waters, because they were made bitter."*

She had seen the rivers turn. She had heard the reports of people dying, their bodies wracked with pain from the poisoned water. The word had spread quickly, panic rippling through the city as people realized that their most basic need—their water—had become a source of death. Rachel had known what it was the moment she heard it. Wormwood. The prophecy unfolding, just as God had said it would.

And yet, here she was, untouched. Protected. God had marked her, sealed her, and she knew it. She could feel it in the depth of her soul, that unshakable certainty that no matter what happened, she was safe in His hands. The fire, the poison, the darkness—they couldn't touch her spirit. She was His.

But that didn't mean she could be complacent.

Rachel stood again, moving to her knees, bowing her head in prayer. She prayed for the people outside her window, the ones who were running in fear, who didn't understand what was happening. She prayed for her church, for the believers who were scattered across the city, facing the same trials and destruction but holding fast to their faith. She prayed for strength, for endurance, for the courage to stand firm in these final days.

And she prayed for Caleb.

Her heart ached for him, for the doubt and fear she had seen in his eyes the last time they spoke. He was so close to the truth, but still holding on to his disbelief, clinging to the idea that somehow, humanity could fix this on its own. She had seen his pride, his refusal to surrender to the faith he had once mocked. But now, as the world crumbled, she could only hope that he would see. That he would finally open his heart to the truth.

"Lord, save him," she whispered, her voice breaking. "I know You're calling to him. I know You're waiting for him. Please, Lord, don't let him be lost."

She stayed there on her knees for a long time, the prayers pouring out of her like a steady stream, each one lifting her spirit higher even as the world outside grew darker. She felt a sense of purpose, a mission to keep praying, to keep standing firm, even as the wrath of God raged around her. This was her role in these final days—to intercede for those who hadn't yet come to God, to stand in the gap and plead for their salvation.

The ground rumbled again, a low, menacing tremor that shook the foundation of her building. The windows rattled in their frames, and for a moment, the candle on her nightstand flickered wildly, threatening to go out. But Rachel didn't flinch. She kept her eyes closed, her hands folded in prayer, her heart steady.

This was the wrath of God. It was His judgment on a world that had rejected Him. But it was also a call to repentance. A final warning, a last chance for those who were willing to open their hearts.

She could feel the weight of it, the urgency, but it didn't crush her. It fueled her. She knew that there were still people out there—people like Caleb—who needed to see, to understand.

And she would keep praying for them, even if the world continued to fall apart around her.

Rachel opened her eyes, feeling the warmth of the candlelight against her face. She took a deep breath, her heart swelling with both sorrow and hope. There was still time, even as the destruction continued. There was still time for repentance, for redemption.

And she would be there, on her knees, praying for it until the very end.

19

SPIRITUAL WARFARE

Rachel knelt by her bed, her hands clasped so tightly in prayer that her knuckles were white. She whispered her prayers softly, though the weight of each word felt as heavy as the world outside her window. The air in the room was thick with tension, the atmosphere almost crackling with the unseen battle she knew was raging just beyond her senses. She could feel it—the presence of something dark, malevolent, creeping around the edges of reality. But just as strongly, she felt the presence of God, steady and unmoving, like a fortress around her soul.

She had known this moment would come, had seen the signs, felt the warnings deep in her spirit. And now, as she prayed, she understood the nature of what was happening. This wasn't just physical destruction. This wasn't just the world falling apart. It was spiritual. The forces of darkness were no longer hidden in the shadows—they were out in the open, tearing through the world with a vengeance.

Outside, she could hear the faint, ominous hum of the locusts, their wings buzzing with a sound that seemed to pierce through the air, through the walls of her apartment. They were everywhere now, tormenting those who had not been sealed by God, driving people to madness with their relentless attacks. She had seen the aftermath herself, had witnessed people writhing in agony on the streets, their faces contorted in pain, their voices hoarse from screaming. It was unbearable to watch, but she knew that their suffering was only temporary, a torment of the flesh. What mattered was their souls.

Rachel's heart ached for them, for the people who had not turned to God, who were now enduring this nightmare. But she also knew that the believers, those who had placed their trust in Christ, were being protected. Their bodies might suffer, but their souls were sealed. She had seen it in their eyes—the strength, the peace that came from knowing they were held by God, even as the world descended into chaos.

She had felt that same peace settle over her, even now, as the world crumbled around her. It was a peace that defied the fear, the terror, and the confusion outside. It was the kind of peace that could only come from knowing that her soul was safe, that no matter what happened next, she belonged to God.

But the battle was far from over.

She understood now that this was more than just physical destruction. This was spiritual warfare—the forces of darkness fighting with all they had, trying to drag as many souls as they could into despair, into rebellion, before the return of Christ. It was the final battle, the one that had been spoken of in scripture, and Rachel knew she had a part to play. Her role wasn't to fight with swords or with might, but to fight in prayer.

She had been preparing for this her whole life, though she hadn't fully realized it until now. Every prayer she had whispered, every verse she had memorized, every time she had called on the name of the Lord—it had all been leading to this moment. The world was under siege, but Rachel knew that the real battle was being fought in the spiritual realm, where angels and demons clashed over the souls of humanity.

Her mind turned to the believers she knew—her church, her friends, the people she had prayed with and for over the years. She could feel their struggles, feel the weight of the darkness pressing in on them. But she also knew they were strong. They had been sealed by God, and that seal was unbreakable. Still, the temptation to give in to fear, to despair, would be overwhelming. And that was why she needed to pray. Now, more than ever.

"Lord, strengthen them," Rachel whispered, her voice filled with urgency. "Give them the courage to stand firm. Protect their minds, protect their hearts. Let them feel Your presence with them, even in the midst of this torment."

Her thoughts drifted to Caleb again, and her heart clenched. She didn't know where he was, didn't know if he had survived the locusts' attacks, but she prayed for him nonetheless. He was still fighting, she could feel it—the battle for his soul was fierce, and he was caught in the middle of it. She prayed that he would have the strength to see through the darkness, that he would finally open his heart to God before it was too late.

"Lord, please, don't let him be lost," she whispered, her voice breaking. "Bring him to You. Break through his pride, through his fear. Let him see You."

The tears that had been threatening to spill over finally did, and Rachel let them fall. The weight of the world's suffering, the agony of the people she loved, and the knowledge of the battle being fought all around her—it was almost too much to bear. But she didn't stop praying. She couldn't.

This was what it meant to be in spiritual warfare. It wasn't about standing on the sidelines, watching as the world fell apart. It was about fighting in the spirit, battling on her knees, calling on the power of God to move, to protect, to save.

"Father, in Your name, I come against every force of darkness that is attacking Your people," Rachel said, her voice growing stronger, more resolute. "I bind the enemy's lies, the fear, the despair. I declare Your victory over this world, over every soul that belongs to You. The enemy has no power here. Your will be done, Lord. Your kingdom come."

Her hands tightened into fists, her eyes closed as she felt the power of her prayers rising. She wasn't alone in this battle—she knew that. The angels were fighting alongside her, the saints were praying across the world, and God Himself was leading the charge. This was His battle, and she was a soldier in His army.

She could feel the darkness pressing in, trying to suffocate her, trying to break her spirit, but it didn't matter. The darkness was no match for the light of God's truth, for the power of His name. And as she continued to pray, she felt that light burning brighter within her, filling her with a strength she hadn't known she had.

The locusts' buzzing grew louder, closer, but Rachel didn't flinch. Her faith was a shield, a weapon, and she wielded it with everything she had. She would not be shaken.

The battle was far from over, but Rachel knew that victory was already assured. Christ was coming. The world was groaning in the final throes of judgment, but He was coming, and when He did, the darkness would be vanquished forever.

Until that day, she would keep fighting.

On her knees, with her hands raised, with every breath and every word of prayer, Rachel would fight. And she would not stop.

20

Despair

C aleb stood in the middle of what was once a city, but now, it resembled something out of a nightmare. The streets were fractured, jagged with cracks from the earthquakes that had torn through the earth, leaving skyscrapers reduced to heaps of twisted steel and broken glass. Fires still smoldered in the distance, the smoke hanging thick and acrid in the air, while the smell of burning and death permeated every breath he took. The sky above, once the serene blue of endless possibility, was now a sickly, churning mass of clouds, lit with flashes of violent lightning that cracked through the atmosphere.

Everything was gone. The world as he had known it, the things he had once relied on—money, government, science—had crumbled into dust, leaving him standing alone amidst the ruins. His mind could barely process it. The banks had collapsed, the markets disintegrated, and the symbols of power that had once ruled society were nothing more than rubble at his feet. The authorities, the leaders, the so-called experts—they had all fallen silent. There were no more answers, no more solutions. There was only chaos.

Caleb had always believed in reason. He had placed his faith in the structures of man, in the systems that kept the world moving. But now, those systems had turned to ash. He had been taught his whole life that humanity was resilient, that no matter how bad things got, they could always rebuild, always rise from the ashes. But this? This wasn't something you could come back from. This was the end, and Caleb knew it.

His hands trembled as he walked, his footsteps echoing hollowly in the desolate street. There was no one left—at least, no one that mattered. The few survivors he passed were hollow-eyed, their faces streaked with dirt and desperation. They huddled in corners, clutching what little they had left, but there was nothing to save them. Not anymore. The government was gone. The money they once fought for had become meaningless paper, scattered in the wind. Science, the cornerstone of Caleb's belief system, had failed to explain or prevent the destruction that had unfolded before his eyes.

He had watched the world fall apart, piece by piece, and with it, his sense of control had vanished. The plagues, the earthquakes, the hailstones the size of boulders that had pummeled the earth—none of it made sense, at least not in the way he had always tried to understand the world. It was like living in a nightmare, one that no amount of logic could wake him from. And now, with everything destroyed, he had nothing left.

He felt lost. Utterly, completely lost.

There was no place for him in this new world, this wasteland that had been carved out of what used to be civilization. Everything he had once believed in had collapsed around him, leaving him adrift, without purpose, without hope. His whole life, he had prided himself on being independent, on not needing anything or anyone, least of all God. But now, in this broken world, the silence of his disbelief was deafening.

Caleb clenched his fists, his breath shaky as he stopped in the middle of the street, staring up at the broken skyline. He felt like screaming, but there was no point. The world had already screamed, and no one had answered. The heavens, once filled with stars and the promise of understanding, had become a battleground of storms and judgment. The air was thick with the weight of it, pressing down on him, suffocating him.

He had always thought that the end would be something he could understand, something he could prepare for. But this? This was something else entirely. It was chaos. It was destruction. It was the very fabric of the world tearing itself apart, and he was standing in the middle of it, powerless to stop it.

For the first time in his life, Caleb was truly afraid.

Not just of the physical destruction, though that was terrifying enough. He was afraid of what it all meant. Afraid that maybe, just maybe, the things Rachel had said were true. Afraid that this was exactly what the prophets had foretold—that the world was being judged, and he was one of the lost. The thought twisted in his gut like a knife, sharp and unrelenting. He had always dismissed the idea of divine judgment, of God's wrath, but now, standing in the ruins of his world, he couldn't shake the feeling that he was being crushed under the weight of something far bigger than himself.

He had refused to turn to God when things had started to fall apart. Even as the judgments began to rain down, even as the witnesses had risen from the dead and ascended into the heavens, Caleb had clung to his disbelief. He had told himself that it was a trick, that there had to be some kind of scientific explanation, that humanity would find a way through. But now, with the ground split open beneath him and the sky threatening to tear apart above him, all he had left was the cold, gnawing emptiness of his own doubt.

He shook his head, his jaw clenched. No. He couldn't accept it. He *wouldn't* accept it. He wasn't one of them. He wasn't one of those people who clung to faith because they were too afraid to face the truth. He had spent his life building something real, something tangible. Science. Knowledge. Control. And now it was all gone.

The despair was suffocating. It wrapped itself around him like a fog, heavy and thick, making it hard to breathe. He wanted to run, to scream, to lash out at something, but there was nothing left to fight against. Nothing except himself.

His heart pounded in his chest, each beat heavy with the weight of hopelessness. He could feel it—the creeping sensation that he was completely and utterly alone, that there was no one coming to save him, no solution waiting in the wings. The world had been judged, and he was part of the wreckage. There was no rebuilding, no coming back from this. The end was here, and he was standing at the edge of it, staring into the abyss.

And yet, even now, even as the darkness closed in around him, Caleb refused to turn to God.

He couldn't. It wasn't pride anymore—it was something deeper, something more ingrained. He had spent too long convincing himself that he didn't need God, that he didn't need anyone, that the world was something he could navigate on his own terms.

To turn back now, to reach out to a God he had spent his life mocking, felt like an admission of defeat too great to bear.

So, he didn't.

Instead, he let the despair wash over him, let the emptiness fill him, and waited for the end. The world had fallen, and with it, so had he.

Caleb stood alone in the ruins of what had once been his life, consumed by the crushing weight of hopelessness. And in that darkness, he couldn't see a way out.

Not now. Not ever.

21

The Rapture

1 Thessalonians 4:17

Rachel stood at her window, watching as the world around her collapsed. The distant skyline, once gleaming with lights and bustling with life, had crumbled into nothing more than fractured ruins. Flames flickered on the horizon, devouring what remained of the great city. The air was heavy with smoke, and the earth trembled beneath her feet. Yet, despite the destruction, despite the darkness that seemed to swallow everything, Rachel felt an unshakable peace.

Rachel knew this wasn't just another city falling. This was a modern Babylon—the great city of the world's rebellion against God. The wealth and decadence it had symbolized, the pride and self-sufficiency it had projected—it had all been built on a foundation of false security, on the illusion that humanity could stand apart from its Creator. And now, it had been brought to its knees.

The fires burned hot and fierce, but Rachel's heart remained calm. The destruction before her was not something to fear—it was a confirmation. Everything that had been written, everything foretold in the Scriptures, was unfolding before her eyes.

The fall of Babylon was a sign that the end was near, that the final battle was approaching, and that God's kingdom was soon to be established.

"Come out of her, my people, that ye be not partakers of her sins, and that ye receive not of her plagues," she had read those words countless times, and now, standing in the ash of Babylon's fall, Rachel felt a deep gratitude swell within her. She had listened. She had heeded the call, separating herself from the trappings of the world, from its empty promises and false security. Her treasure was in heaven, and that was all she needed.

Rachel closed her eyes, a prayer rising from her heart, soft and steady. "Thank You, Lord, for Your faithfulness. Thank You for bringing Your word to pass, for showing the world that You are just and true. I know the end is near. I know You are coming."

As she stood there, watching the city burn, Rachel felt an unshakable certainty fill her. The destruction wasn't something to fear—it was a promise fulfilled. God's kingdom was drawing near, and soon, Christ would return.

***

Rachel felt the shift before she saw it—an almost imperceptible pulling, as if the very fabric of her being was drawn toward something beyond the limits of the earth. Her heart raced, not with fear, but with an overwhelming sense of anticipation. This was the moment she had waited for, prayed for, and lived her life in expectation of. The moment that had sustained her through every trial, every tear, and every struggle of faith.

And then, in an instant, it happened.

In an instant, it happened.

The world around her dissolved, the ground beneath her feet losing its hold as the air shimmered with light. Her breath caught as her body began to change—no longer heavy, no longer bound by the limitations of flesh. Her physical form, with all its scars and burdens, faded like a forgotten memory, replaced by something new, something glorified.

Rachel was lifted, caught up into the sky with the other saints. All around her, she could see them—countless believers, their faces radiant with the same awe and joy that filled her own heart. They, too, had shed their earthly forms, their new bodies shining with an inner light. It was a feeling of pure freedom and peace, as though the weight of the world had been left far behind.

The earth, with all its pain and suffering, was beneath her now. The old order of things was passing away, and Rachel's soul soared in the knowledge that she was being drawn closer to the One she had longed for her entire life. She was being lifted into the presence of Christ Himself.

The air around her sparkled with a brilliance that defied description, as if the very atmosphere had been infused with the glory of heaven. Rachel could hardly contain the joy that filled her. Her heart was light, her spirit free, and for the first time, she truly understood what it meant to be made new. Every sorrow, every doubt, every moment of pain was behind her now, and would be washed away in the radiant light of her Savior.

Rachel stood at the edge of the hill, her heart pounding in her chest as she gazed at the sky above. The air shimmered with a brilliance she had never seen before, a light so pure it made her entire being feel weightless. She had always known this day would come, but standing here now, witnessing it with her own eyes, the reality of it took her breath away.

Rachel's hands clasped together, her heart swelling with joy so fierce it felt as though it might burst. Her knees trembled, but she stood tall, rooted in the peace that had carried her through the trials and tribulations of the last days. She had waited for this moment, prayed for it, longed for it, and now, it was here. The return of Christ, the fulfillment of every promise, every prophecy, was unfolding before her eyes.

***

The clouds had parted, and there, descending from the heavens, was Christ, standing at the center of it all.

His presence filled the sky with a radiance that eclipsed the sun itself. Clad in a robe dipped in His sacrificial blood, His eyes blazed like fire, and upon His head were many crowns. Behind Him, the armies of heaven followed, dressed in robes of pure white, their faces illuminated by the glory of the One they served.

His presence brighter than the sun, yet gentle and welcoming. His arms were open wide, and the love that emanated from Him was overwhelming. Rachel's heart leaped at the sight of Him, tears of joy streaming down her face as she felt herself being drawn closer and closer to His presence.

The saints gathered around Him, radiant and glorified, their new bodies a reflection of the perfection they had longed for in the brokenness of their earthly lives. Rachel marveled at the beauty of it all—faces she recognized, believers she had known and loved, all transformed and made whole. There was no more sickness, no more aging, no more pain. They were as they were meant to be, and Rachel felt the peace of that truth settle deep within her soul.

And then, she was there—standing before Christ Himself.

Everything else faded away. His gaze, bright and full of eternity, held her, and yet there was something deeply personal in the way His eyes shone upon her, as though He had known her from the very beginning. His love was so powerful, so consuming, it felt like a tangible presence, wrapping around her and holding her in perfect peace.

Rachel fell to her knees, not from fear, but from the overwhelming sense of reverence that washed over her. She knelt in the grass, her eyes lifted toward the King of kings, her heart bursting with the knowledge that this was the moment she had been waiting for her whole life, her mind overcome by the sheer majesty of the moment. She had waited her whole life for this—this meeting, this homecoming. And now, as she knelt before the King of kings, the Lamb who had been slain, she felt the weight of His grace and mercy wash over her like a flood.

"Well done, good and faithful servant."

His voice was soft, yet it carried the power of heaven and earth. Rachel's heart soared at the sound of it, her tears flowing freely as the reality of those words sank in. She had been faithful. She had trusted Him through every storm, every dark night, and now she was home.

Tears filled her eyes, not of sorrow, but of awe and joy. The world, broken and scarred from the judgments that had fallen upon it, was about to be made new. The pain, the suffering, the darkness—it was all coming to an end. And Rachel, standing in the presence of her King, knew with every fiber of her being that she had remained faithful to the end.

The ground beneath her seemed to pulse with the promise of renewal. The scars of the world, the wounds of creation, would soon be healed. The curse of sin would be no more. And Rachel, along with the other faithful, would step into the New Jerusalem, a place where the light of God would never fade, where they would worship Him forever in perfect peace.

"Behold, I make all things new."

The words echoed in her heart, and Rachel felt a profound peace settle over her. Christ's kingdom was coming. Soon, the New Jerusalem would descend, and they would dwell with God forever. No more sin. No more pain. Only the light of His glory, shining eternally.

The journey was complete. The trials of the old world, the suffering and pain, were behind her now. Before her stretched eternity—an eternity spent in the presence of the One who had redeemed her. There was no more sorrow, no more death. All things had been made new.

As the saints gathered around the throne, lifting their voices in worship, Rachel knew that this was home. This was where she had always been meant to be—caught up with Christ, glorified and whole, living in the eternal light of His love.

Her story was no longer one of struggle or sorrow, but one of eternal peace, as she walked with her Savior forever.

22

The Lamb's Book of Life

Revelation 20: 11-15

Caleb's entire body trembled as he stood before the great white throne. His legs were unsteady, weak beneath him, as if they might give way at any moment. The light that radiated from the One seated on the throne was unlike anything he had ever known—too pure, too powerful. It pierced through him, reaching into the deepest, darkest corners of his soul, illuminating everything he had ever been, every choice he had ever made. There was nowhere to hide, no part of him left untouched by the brilliance. His heart pounded in his chest, each beat like the pounding of a death knell. He had never felt so small, so helpless.

A sea of faces surrounded him—countless souls standing in the vastness before the throne—but Caleb had never felt more alone. His throat was dry, his hands shook uncontrollably at his sides, and his mind raced, trying desperately to cling to something, anything that could save him. But there was nothing.

The books had been opened.

He had watched it happen, felt the weight of it settle over him like a crushing boulder. First, the book of deeds—the record of every thought, every word, every action, laid out for all to see.

And as the pages turned, as the details of his life were revealed, Caleb could feel his heart sinking deeper into despair.

His life—so carefully constructed, so proudly built on intellect, on strength, on self-reliance—was now exposed for what it truly was: a testament to arrogance and rebellion. He had denied God at every turn, laughed in the face of faith, believing that he had all the time in the world to figure things out, to make his choice. He had mocked the very idea that faith mattered, convinced that his own reasoning could carry him through.

And now, all of it—the defiance, the rejection, the pride—was being laid bare.

The voice of the One seated on the throne rang out like thunder, shaking Caleb to his core. It wasn't just a voice—it was the embodiment of truth and justice, and it echoed through his entire being, leaving no room for denial or excuse.

> *"Your deeds have been weighed.*
> *Your heart has been judged."*

Caleb's breath caught in his throat. The sound of the pages turning was unbearable, like the ticking of a clock counting down the final moments of his life. He could feel his hands clenching into fists at his sides, his nails digging into his palms, but it did nothing to stop the trembling. He wanted to cry out, to beg for mercy, but the weight of his guilt choked the words before they could reach his lips.

He knew what was coming.

The Lamb's Book of Life was opened, and Caleb's heart raced, wild with desperation. He searched the faces of those standing before the throne, looked for any sign that maybe—just maybe—his name would be found within its pages. That somehow, through some miracle, there might still be grace for him. He thought of Rachel, of her endless prayers, her unwavering faith. Maybe her love, her pleading had been enough.

But the silence stretched out before him like an endless chasm. His name was not there.

The realization struck him with the force of a thousand regrets, each one cutting deeper than the last. His heart sank, and a hollow, empty ache filled his chest. He had rejected every opportunity—every time God had reached out to him, he had turned away. He had chosen pride over repentance, arrogance over surrender. And now, as the truth of it all crashed down on him, he knew without a doubt that it was too late.

The finality of it was crushing. It settled over him like a weight that he could never escape.

The One on the throne spoke again, His voice filled with sorrow and justice, a judgment that Caleb could not outrun.

> *"And whosoever was not found written in the book of life was cast into the lake of fire."—(Revelation 20:15)*

The ground beneath Caleb's feet gave way, and he felt his knees buckle beneath him. The words echoed in his mind, each syllable driving deeper into his soul, tearing at him with relentless force. He had missed it. His chance, his time—it was over. There would be no more moments of decision, no more chances to turn back. The door had closed, and there was nothing left but regret.

The verdict was spoken, clear and undeniable.

> *"Depart from Me, ye cursed, into everlasting fire, prepared for the devil and his angels."—(Matthew 25:41)*

The words hit Caleb like a death sentence, but this was worse than death. This was eternal. His legs gave out beneath him, and he fell to the ground, his hands trembling as they clutched the earth. The weight of eternal separation pressed down on him like a suffocating shroud. It was a finality that he had never imagined, an unrelenting torment that left no room for hope. He had rejected God's mercy, refused to bow, and now the price was being paid in full.

Tears streamed down his face, hot and bitter, but they brought no relief, no redemption. Only the choking sorrow of regret. His heart screamed for another chance, for one more moment to make a different choice, to undo all the times he had turned away—but there was none.

The darkness rose up around him, overwhelming, suffocating. He could feel it—could feel the chasm opening beneath his feet, the lake of fire waiting to consume him. The heat of it, the despair of it, the knowledge that this was the end and there would be no reprieve, no release, no escape.

As the light of the throne began to fade from his view, replaced by the overwhelming darkness of eternal separation, Caleb's cries were swallowed by the void. The weight of his choices, the arrogance that had kept him from the truth, would now be his torment forever.

The fire that awaited him wasn't just physical—it was the agony of knowing, without a shadow of a doubt, that he had rejected the only source of life, the only hope of salvation. He had clung to his pride, refused to surrender, and now, the weight of that refusal would haunt him for all eternity.

His name was not written in the Book of Life.

23

Tribulation

Caleb's breath came in ragged gasps as the darkness closed in around him. The words echoed in his mind, sharp and relentless:

"Depart from Me, ye cursed, into everlasting fire."

His legs had given out beneath him, his hands clutching at the earth that seemed to slip away beneath his fingers. His heart raced, his chest tight with the suffocating weight of regret, as the fiery abyss opened before him.

The lake of fire waited, its flames roaring with the agony of a thousand lifetimes. His screams were silent, swallowed by the void. The darkness rose, consuming him, and he fell—endlessly, helplessly—into the fiery torment below.

Suddenly, Caleb bolted upright, his chest heaving, his body drenched in sweat. The nightmare was still fresh in his mind, the terror still clutching at his heart. He gasped for air, his hands trembling as he wiped the sweat from his brow. His mouth was dry, parched as if the heat of the nightmare had followed him into the waking world. His heart hammered in his chest as he looked around his dimly lit bedroom, the faint glow of the streetlight filtering through the blinds.

Just a dream. Just a nightmare. But why had it felt so real?

His throat felt tight, and he needed water—*now.* Caleb swung his legs out of bed and stumbled to the kitchen, his bare feet slapping against the cold tile floor. He yanked open the fridge, grabbing the bottle of ice water he always kept there. He gulped it down, the cold liquid soothing his dry throat, but his hands still shook, and the gnawing pit of dread in his stomach refused to fade.

That dream... No, it wasn't just a dream. It had been more than that—something else, something dark. The flames, the judgment, the finality of it all. His chest tightened again, and he forced himself to focus on the coolness of the water. It was just a nightmare. Just a horrible dream.

But then his phone buzzed loudly from the counter, pulling him back to reality. It buzzed again. And again.

Nonstop.

Caleb frowned, walking over to the counter and grabbing his phone. His hands were still shaking, but this time it wasn't from the dream. His screen was flooded with notifications—news alerts, messages, missed calls. His thumb hovered over the screen for a moment, dread pooling in his gut as the buzzing continued.

And then he heard it.

Outside, beyond the walls of his quiet apartment, emergency sirens screamed through the night. The low wail of them cut through the eerie stillness, and Caleb's blood ran cold.

He unlocked his phone, swiping through the barrage of alerts. The first message was from a news app:

> **BREAKING:** Millions of people have died worldwide from mysterious, sudden causes. Deaths reported began at exactly midnight. Authorities scrambling to understand cause. UN in emergency meetings.

His heart stuttered in his chest as he read the headline, and he quickly scrolled to the next alert:

> Global death toll in the millions—UN confirms deaths primarily among Christians. New global leader assumes power as many world leaders confirmed dead.

His breath caught in his throat, and his fingers flew over the screen, swiping to the next news report. His mind raced as the words blurred together. *Millions* had died—*Christians*. His pulse quickened, and a cold sweat broke out along the back of his neck. *Christians?* That's what they all had in common?

He blinked at the screen, his heart pounding louder than the sirens outside. His nightmare clung to him like a shadow, and a creeping sense of dread began to spread through him. The pieces started to fall into place—the nightmare, the deaths, the fact that it was Christians. He swallowed hard, his mind reeling.

He quickly dialed his mom's number, his fingers trembling. The phone rang and rang, each ring a hammer blow to his chest. She didn't answer. Panic surged through him as he tried his brother next—*nothing*. His fingers fumbled as he tried Rachel's number—no answer.

The room began to spin, the walls pressing in on him. He dialed again. His mother, his brother, Rachel—all of them unreachable.

Finally, he tried his father's number, his heart thudding painfully in his chest. The phone barely rang once before it picked up.

"Dad?" Caleb's voice was shaky, breathless.

There was a long, heavy silence on the other end, and for a moment, Caleb thought the call had dropped. But then, he heard it—his father's ragged breathing, followed by quiet sobs.

"Caleb," his father's voice cracked, broken with grief. "They're gone. Your mother... your brother... they're... gone."

The room tilted, and Caleb staggered back, gripping the counter for support. The phone nearly slipped from his grasp as his father's words sank in.

"No... no, no, no... Dad, what do you mean?" Caleb's voice was a frantic whisper, his mind spinning. "What do you mean they're gone?"

"I... I woke up and... they were just... gone," his father choked, his sobs breaking through the words. "They're dead, Caleb. Both of them."

The nightmare crashed back into his mind, the flames, the judgment, the finality of it all. His mother had warned him. Rachel had tried to tell him. And now... now they were gone, and it was too late.

His phone buzzed again, and Caleb's gaze dropped to the screen, barely able to focus through the fog of panic and disbelief. A live news feed appeared, and Caleb tapped it instinctively, his hands shaking so badly he could barely hold the phone.

On the screen, a sharply dressed man stood at a podium, his face calm and authoritative as he addressed the world. Behind him, the flags of nations flapped in the breeze. The man's voice echoed through the phone, calm and measured.

"In light of the recent events and the tragic loss of millions of lives worldwide, we must act swiftly to protect our citizens and maintain order. Effective immediately, every individual will be issued an identification chip, to be implanted in the wrist, which will allow for the regulation of commerce and ensure the safety of all."

Caleb's breath caught in his throat, and the phone slipped from his grasp, clattering to the floor.

The ID chip. The ability to buy and sell. *Everything* his mother had warned him about. The words from her Bible came rushing back—the ones he'd dismissed, the ones he'd laughed at.

The mark.

The weight of it all hit him at once. The deaths, the nightmare, the world collapsing around him. It was all true. Everything she had said, everything she had begged him to understand.

His legs gave out, and Caleb slumped to the floor, burying his face in his hands as despair washed over him.

His mother had been right.

It was all happening.

And now, there was nothing he could do.

To be continued...

Dear Reader,

Thank you for journeying through *Edge of Oblivion*. As you've seen, Caleb believed he had all the time in the world. He leaned on his own intellect, his strength, and dismissed faith as something to consider later. But when the moment of reckoning came, Caleb realized—too late—that the decisions he made in life sealed his fate for eternity. His regret was overwhelming, but by then, it was irreversible.

Rachel, on the other hand, stood firm in her unwavering faith, even as the world around her crumbled. She believed in the promise of redemption and remained steadfast until the end. When the time came, her past was forgotten, cast into the sea of forgetfulness, and her reward was eternal peace. She was taken up with Christ in the Rapture, to live forever in the New Jerusalem, where sorrow and pain no longer exist.

We each are faced with a choice. One day, we will all stand before the ultimate judgment. There will be no more excuses, no more second chances. You will either hear the comforting words, *"Well done, good and faithful servant,"* or the heartbreaking declaration, *"Depart from Me, I never knew you."*

The end is coming, whether we want to face it or not. This story serves as a vivid reminder that waiting for tomorrow to make your choice is the greatest risk of all. The time to decide is now. Will you embrace the opportunity to have your sins forgiven, to have your past cast into the sea of forgetfulness, and be welcomed into eternity with open arms? Or will you hesitate until it's too late, left standing in regret?

If this story has touched you, I encourage you to take the next step: pray the prayer on the following pages with sincerity and share Christ and this book with others. Don't let this message stop with you—there are many who need to hear it and be reminded that the time for choice is now.

Tomorrow may be too late.

> If you declare with your mouth, "Jesus is Lord," and believe in your heart that God raised him from the dead, you will be saved. For it is with your heart that you believe and are justified, and it is with your mouth that you profess your faith and are saved.
>
> (Romans 10:9-10, NIV)

Sincerely,

Abiegail Rose
Author of *Edge of Oblivion*

SALVATION

If you believe the Bible offers the truth about the way to salvation, but you have not taken the step to become a Christian, it's as simple as praying this prayer. You can pray by yourself, using your own words. There is no special formula. Just pray from your heart to God, and He *will* save you. If you feel lost and don't know what to pray, here's a salvation prayer that you can follow:

Dear Lord,

I admit that I am a sinner. I have done many things that don't please you. I have lived my life for myself only. I am sorry, and I repent. I ask you to forgive me. I believe that you died on the cross for me, to save me. You did what I could not do for myself. I come to you now and ask you to take control of my life; I give it to you. From this day forward, help me to live every day for you and in a way that pleases you. I love you, Lord, and I thank you that I will spend all eternity with you.

In Jesus' Name,
Amen.

ABIEGAIL ROSE
FROM OBLIVION ONTO
GLORY

From Oblivion onto Glory

The Revelation Chronicles Book 2

Caleb thought he had escaped his nightmare, but when millions of Christians mysteriously die and a new world order rises, he realizes his darkest fears are only just beginning. Now, caught in the Tribulation, he finds himself battling forces far beyond anything he imagined—and his greatest enemy may be himself.

As the world falls under the iron grip of a new leader, Caleb discovers a purpose that pushes him to the edge of faith and beyond. Using his skills as a programmer, he infiltrates the global social media systems, sharing the gospel with those still searching for hope. But in a world where every move is monitored and every message controlled, his mission becomes increasingly dangerous.

Caleb faces a choice: continue hiding in the shadows or risk everything to stand for the truth—even if it means paying the ultimate price. Yet, even death may not be the end, because beyond the chaos, beyond the suffering, lies the promise of something greater: where all things are made new.

Can Caleb rise from the ashes of oblivion and become a beacon of light in the darkest of times? Or will he fall into the hands of those who seek to destroy the truth?

Pre-order *From Oblivion onto Glory* today by visiting Books2Read.com/OblivionOntoGlory and follow Caleb's harrowing journey through the Tribulation. Secure your copy now and be among the first to experience the gripping sequel to *Edge of Oblivion*—a story of faith, courage, and the eternal battle between light and darkness.

Don't wait—eternity is at stake.

Visit www.books2read.com/oblivionontoglory to reserve your copy today!

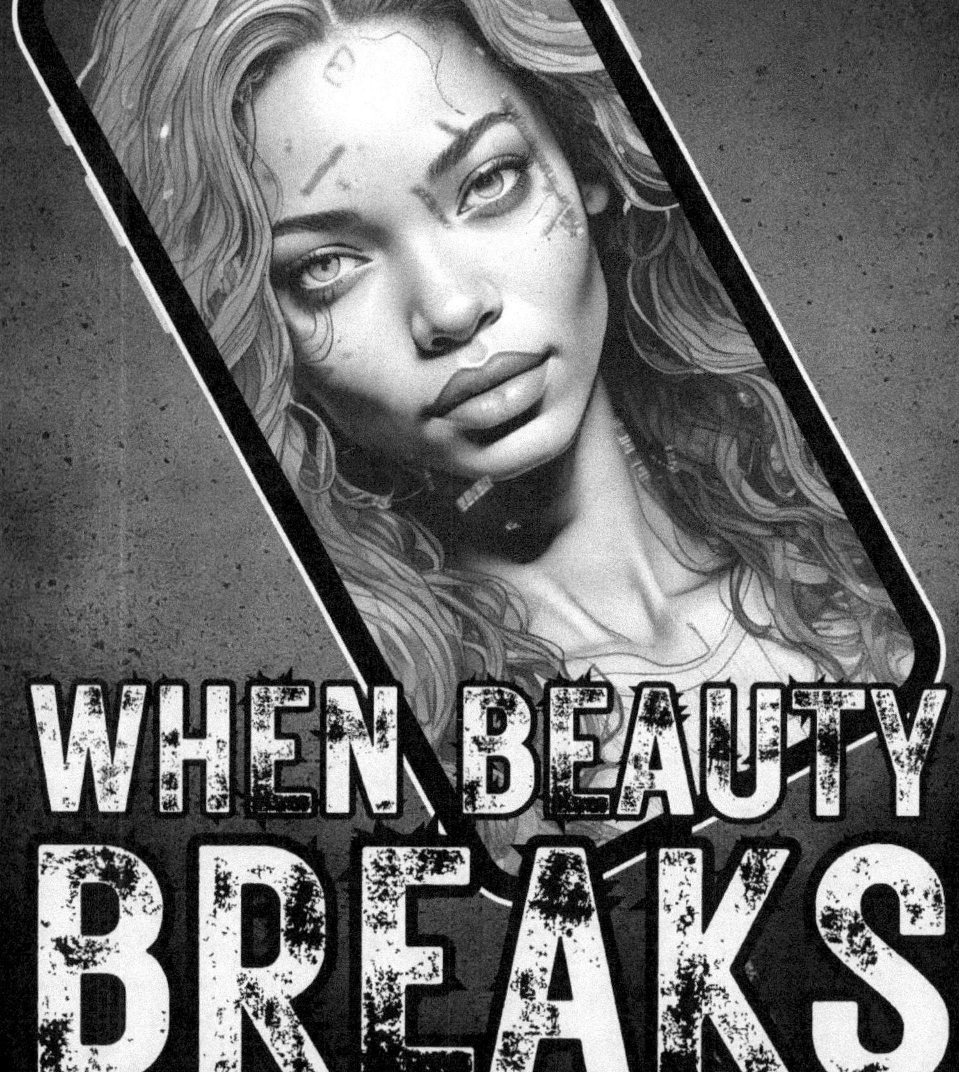

BY ABIEGAIL ROSE
WHEN BEAUTY BREAKS
A PSYCHOSPIRITUAL PARANORMAL THRILLER

When Beauty Breaks

A Psychospiritual Paranormal Thriller

"When beauty becomes a curse, fame is the price I can no longer afford."

Beauty is fleeting. This was a truth woven into the fabric of my upbringing, like the delicate threads of a cherished family tapestry. I remember my mother's gentle voice, barely audible over the hum of the Sunday morning congregation, as she whispered those words like a persistent prayer.

"Remember, sweetheart, beauty is fleeting."

My mother believed it with all her heart. She lived by it. But I... I didn't listen.

I was too focused on the reflection in the mirror, captivated by the shimmering image of perfection that stared back at me. I craved the compliments, the instant gratification of a hundred likes on social media, and those ephemeral moments when people saw me and thought I was someone worth admiring.

Somewhere along that path, I traded in my mother's whispers for the thunderous applause of the world. Faith surrendered to fame; my soul was sacrificed for beauty.

This is a story about how that choice destroyed me.

But it's not just about vanity. It's about control—about wanting to be more than what I am, to be seen, adored, praised. It's about the insatiable yearning that gnaws away at one's very being until everything else—morals, relationships, identity—is stripped away like dead leaves in a storm.

It's about making a deal with dark forces for eternal youth and beauty only to see that desire twist and decay until all that remains is an empty reflection.

Because beauty is fragile. For all its power, it doesn't last. And once you've sold your soul for it, there's no going back—or so I thought.

Before you read this story, remember: Not everything that glitters is gold. Sometimes, it hides something far darker beneath its seductive surface.

Pre-Order Today on Barnes & Noble, Amazon and other Major Retailers by visiting Books2Read.com/WhenBeautyBreaks

What People Are Saying...

"When Beauty Breaks is a haunting and emotionally charged novel that echoes the timeless themes of Oscar Wilde's The Picture of Dorian Gray while plunging deep into the modern world of social media, celebrity, and the fragile pursuit of perfection."

"A modern-day gothic masterpiece."

"Abiegail brilliantly captures the dark side of modern beauty culture, crafting a story that feels like a cautionary tale for our times."

"A gripping meditation on the dangers of vanity and the fleeting nature of social media-driven fame."

Pre-Order Today on Barnes & Noble, Amazon and other Major Retailers by visiting Books2Read.com/WhenBeautyBreaks

About the Author

Abiegail Rose

Abiegail Rose is an author known for weaving tales of passion, heartache, and ultimate triumph. With a gift for creating unforgettable characters and immersive stories, Abiegail's novels have captured the hearts of readers around the globe, earning her a loyal following.

Born with a love for storytelling, Abiegail began her writing journey at a young age, filling notebooks with tales of romance and adventure. Her unique ability to tap into the emotional depths of her characters has made her a standout voice in the romance genre, with each book exploring the complexities of love in its many forms.

In addition to her success as an author, Abiegail has a background in marketing, where she discovered the powerful parallels between crafting compelling love stories and creating engaging brand narratives. This realization inspired her to write *Love Lessons in Marketing: How Love Story Tropes Can Elevate Your Brand Strategy*, blending her two passions into a guide that helps brands connect with their audiences on a deeply emotional level.

When she's not writing, Abiegail enjoys traveling, indulging in classic romance novels, and exploring the latest trends in marketing and storytelling. She lives with her family in the Houston-Metro, where she continues to dream up new stories that inspire, entertain, and remind us all of the power of love.

Want to join her book club to be first in line for new releases? Visit https://authorabiegailrose.com/

Follow her on Instagram @authorabiegailrose

Follow her on Goodreads
https://www.goodreads.com/abiegailrose

Follow her on Amazon
http://amazon.com/author/abiegailrose

Get a signed book: http://authorabiegailrose.com

Also by Abiegail Rose

<u>Thrillers & Suspense</u>

When Beauty Breaks: A Psychospiritual Paranormal Thriller

Edge of Oblivion

Oblivion onto Glory

Armored in Faith – Coming December

<u>Sweet & Clean Romance</u>

Ace's Heart: An Ex-Mafia, 2ndChance, Christian Romance

Cupcakes & Romance

Love & Decay: A Zombpocalypse Romance (Kindle Vella)

<u>Motivational</u>

Let Your Light Shine : Rocking Your Purpose, Living Your Passion

Blessed Nourishment Vol. 1

49 Days of Self-Discovery

Prince, Not Required: Slaying your inner dragons, without dropping your crown!

<u>Business</u>

Love Lessons in Marketing: How Love Story Tropes Can Elevate
Your Brand
Boss Babe Publishing: The Ultimate Self-Publishing Guide and
Workbook
The Carter Effect: Hip-Hop 101
Boss Babe by Design

Children's Books

Duke's Puppy Manners Series
The Lost Chronicles of Light Series

www.ingramcontent.com/pod-product-compliance
Lightning Source LLC
Chambersburg PA
CBHW071156300726
48975CB00004B/1179